I0633034

BLOODY CANAAN

ROGUE LAWMAN EIGHT

PETER BRANDVOLD

WOLFPACK
PUBLISHING
— EST 2013 —

Bloody Canaan
Print Edition
© Copyright 2022 (As Revised) Peter Brandvold

Wolfpack Publishing
5130 S. Fort Apache Rd. 215-380
Las Vegas, NV 89148

wolfpackpublishing.com

Paperback ISBN 978-1-63977-086-1

BLOODY CANAAN

JACOB BROYLES LOOKED ABRUPTLY UP FROM THE rabbit-skin mittens he was finishing sewing at the kitchen table, and turned toward the window beside him. He cast his pale blind eyes to his older sister. "Trouble, Jennie."

Jennie Broyles turned away from the pot she'd been stirring on the range. "Oh, hell—what now?"

Her younger sister, Mercy, gasped. "Jennie, what has Pa told you about that blue tongue of yours!"

"Pa's in bed, so I'm the one in charge, and you'd best get used to my blue tongue," Jennie said as she made her way around the table. "I'll cuss when I feel like cussin'. If you don't like it, little Miss Mercy, you'd best stuff your ears."

Mercy looked at their brother in shock and sighed. Jacob gave a devilish grin.

"Don't let her pull you down to hell with her!" Mercy scolded her older brother.

Jacob was sixteen. Mercy was thirteen. At nineteen, Jennie was the oldest of the three Broyles siblings. If a girl could be at once radiantly and earthily beautiful, that was Jennie. Which made her salty tongue all the more shocking to most who knew her.

Jennie swept a curtain aside and looked out through the dusty sashed panes, turning her head this way and that as she scoured the yard of the small mountain ranch with her gaze.

"I don't see anything."

"Me, neither," Mercy said. She'd gotten up from her chair at the table to peer over Jennie's left shoulder.

"Riders," Jacob said, staring straight ahead across the table littered with his tanning tools, at the canvas of mountain wildflowers Jennie had painted earlier that summer. He wasn't seeing the painting or anything else. A severe fever had taken his vision when he was five years old.

"Seven, maybe eight horses," Jacob said in a dull monotone. "They're comin' fast."

A chill ran down Jennie's spine. She didn't doubt her brother's judgment about such things. He may have lost his vision, but his other senses had grown keener to compensate. Jennie looked across the ranch yard to the rail corral abutting the barn.

Several horses were looking to the south and twitching their ears. The chestnut gelding Jennie called Whisper pawed nervously at the dirt, arching its tail.

Jennie's heartbeat quickened. Her hands grew clammy.

"Burnett," Jacob whispered, awfully.

"Oh, my god!" Mercy cried, and clapped both hands to her mouth

"He said he'd come," Jacob said, the dullness in his voice belying his own fear. "So, now he's come." He turned toward Jennie, his blind eyes looking past her to the window. "What're you gonna do, sis?"

Jennie drew a calming breath as she walked over to where her father's Sharps carbine rested on wooden pegs above the fireplace.

"You two get upstairs, and stay there till I tell you to come down." The Sharps was loaded. As Jennie held it in both hands, barrel up, breathing hard now with fear, she gave Mercy a direct look. "For god's sakes, keep Poppa up there—you hear, Mercy? Don't you dare let him get out of bed—no matter what he hears outside."

"What're you gonna do, Jennie?" Mercy's voice was small and trembling as she stared at the rifle in her sister's arms. "What're you gonna do?"

"Just do as I say, dammit, Mercy!"

"I'll try," Mercy said, fear showing in her own wide eyes as she looked out the window, staring at the horses. She slid that glassy gaze to her older sister. "Do you... do you really think it's Burnett? He wouldn't, would he? He really wouldn't?"

"He said he'd come," Jacob said, kicking his chair back as he rose a little unsteadily from the table. "He thinks he can do anything. He thinks he owns the whole range, and... all the folks on it. All the women on it. So... he's come. Who else would be comin' at this time of day, bringing all those riders? We knew he'd come... sooner or later. He said he would, and he always follows through on his threats, Burnett does."

Jennie shot her brother and sister a sharp, commanding look. "Would you two stop your gassin' and get the hell upstairs?"

"Come on, Jacob," Mercy said in that little girl's trembling voice again, taking her brother's hand and leading him up the stairs to the cabin's second story.

No lamps had been lit yet in the cabin, so the interior was all shadows and misty edges. Brassy late-afternoon light shone briefly in Mercy's blond hair as she led Jacob up the stairs, past Jacob's furs and hides stretched from nails in the log wall. The staircase squawked beneath his and his little sister's weight.

When they left the stairs, Jennie could hear them hurrying down the narrow hall up there. Then a door shut with a squawk of hinges, and the bolt was thrown with a metallic thud.

"What's goin' on?" came the phlegmy voice of Angus Broyles from his room on the second story. "It ain't nighttime yet, is it?" A brief pause. "Why, no—it's still light out. Jennie, what's goin'—?"

"Never mind, Pa," Jennie cut her father off. "Just stay up there and keep quiet. They'll be gone in a minute."

"*Who* will?"

Jennie looked out the window once more, then walked to the door. As she wrapped her hand around the doorknob, she drew a deep, calming breath—which didn't really calm her much at all—and then drew the door quickly open and stepped onto the stoop.

"You can go to hell, Quentin Burnett," she muttered to herself, trying to bring up as much anger as the fear she felt. She had every right to be angry. To be furious, in fact. Burnett's demands were not only unreasonable but illegal. However, it was mostly fear Jennie was feeling now. "You can go to *hell*, Quentin Burnett," she said again as she turned her gaze to the south.

The wooden ranch portal straddling the two-track trail at the edge of the ranch yard almost perfectly framed the group of riders galloping toward her, dust rising behind them touched with the salmons and burnt oranges of the mountain sunset.

The hoof thuds grew louder as the men rode under the portal and continued into the yard.

Jennie's hands turned cold when she saw the group was led by the notorious Texas gunfighter, Vance Dodge, who was Quentin Burnett's first lieutenant. Dodge ramrodded all the beating, killing, and hanging Burnett inflicted on those he considered illegally nesting on government range—free range that Burnett wrongfully, illegally, considered his own.

Jennie's gaze fluttered across the dusty riders drawing up in the yard before her, about twenty feet away. Quentin Burnett himself was not among them.

Vance Dodge was leading the group alone.

Dodge's eyes were cold and dark beneath the brim of his dark gray Stetson. He was a rangy, bearded man with long, dark-brown hair curling onto the collar of his duster. He wore a silver hoop ring in his right ear, and he had a scar in the shape of a large fishhook on his left cheek. Without the scar and the cruelty in his small eyes, he would have been a man whom Jennie might call handsome.

His double shell belts bristled with three big Colt pistols.

The rest of Burnett's group of hard-tailed riders rode behind Dodge.

Jennie recognized all of them, as would most of the other nesters who called this high mountain valley home, and whom Burnett frequently harassed, and whose beef he often stole. A few weeks ago, a "nester" named Emory had been found hanging from a tree on his own range.

Most of the men facing Jennie now had reputations that stretched beyond this remote mountain range. There was the burly Chick Holt and the one-eyed Frank Sunday and the cow-eyed Hacksaw Campbell, who was known more as a tracker than a gunslinger, though

Jennie, who kept her ear to the rails, so to speak, had heard he'd killed several men in Kansas.

There was O.B. "Antelope" Warner who wore a bowler hat and a three-piece suit with checked trousers as well as dark-tinted spectacles. He looked more like a carnival barker than a gunman, but he'd been known for his bloody work in several range wars in Wyoming and Colorado.

The last two riders were the Miller brothers from Oklahoma, whom Jennie had heard had killed the renowned Deputy U.S. Marshal Bill Ruth over in Dakota Territory, after they'd robbed a train. They'd walked into Ruth's house on a little farm outside of Bismarck in the middle of the night, and they'd shot both Ruth and his wife while they'd slept before raping and killing both Ruth daughters.

The story going around the mountains was that the Millers were the only two men Jesse James had ever declined to fight, for both wild-eyed, blood-hungry young men were known to be several cards short of a full deck. Apparently, the folly in their eyes had turned even Jesse James's blood to ice.

The riders spread out in front of the Broyles's log cabin in a broad semicircle, facing Jennie. Their dust caught up to them, billowing this way and that in the yard lit in tones of the early mountain dusk. The men stared dully at Jennie.

Except the Millers, that was. The Miller brothers had greedy, covetous looks in their eyes as they feasted their gazes on the well-set-up young woman before them.

Jennie's eyes flicked to the top of her dress. It had been a hot day, so she'd worn a plain cambric sleeveless affair with a relatively low neckline, which exposed the high slopes of her breasts. Her bosom rose and fell heavily as she breathed against the fear ripping through her body like cold tar.

A cool bead of sweat trickled down her cleavage.

Vance Dodge abruptly removed his hat and held it against his chest. "Good afternoon, Miss Broyles. And how are you today? If you don't mind me sayin' so, you're lookin' splendid."

Antelope Warner turned a sneer on Dodge. "Splendid?"

"Yeah, splendid," Dodge said, defensively. "That was Burnett's word for her. Splendid. He said the very word when he saw her in town a few months back. Splendid. I reckon he couldn't get such a splendid-lookin' creature out of his head. Smitten, the old boy is, sure enough. And that's why we're here, Miss Broyles. But then you already know that—don't you?"

"You can go to hell, Dodge," Jennie said, trying to keep her voice from trembling. "And you can tell Burnett he can go to hell, too!"

"Splendid, is what he called you," Dodge said, smiling, as though he hadn't heard what she'd said. "He said to me today around noon, 'Vance, you take the boys and ride on out to the Broyles ranch and bring me that splendid creature. That Jennie Broyles. I'm gonna marry her.'"

Dodge spread his gloved hands two feet apart. "His smile was that wide!"

Jennie moved to the edge of the porch. She held the Sharps in both hands across her heaving chest. "I'm not goin' anywhere, Dodge. You tell him that. I'd rather marry a diamondback than marry Quentin Burnett."

"No, no, no," Dodge said, grinning and shaking his head. "You don't want me to tell him that. Look, I understand. He's old. He's fat. And he probably has a dick the size of my little finger—and that's fully erect!"

The other men snickered and chuckled.

"But he's the most powerful man in this county. Maybe even in the whole damn territory," Dodge continued. "Why, the governor of Idaho is ridin' to New Canaan tomorrow to go huntin' with the old bastard! Burnett thinks he owns the entire mountain range. Now, we know he don't—it's government range—but you know what happens when you try tellin' him that. In his mind, you see, this is all his range"—he swept his arm out in a broad arc—"includin' your ranch here. Includin' *you* yourself, Miss Broyles. So he's gonna marry you. I'm sorry—it's a real pickle. I know it is. And I'm sorry. But when Burnett says he's gonna do somethin', that's that!"

CHAPTER 2

"I TOLD BURNETT NO!" JENNIE FAIRLY SCREAMED, aiming the Sharps at Dodge, the rifle quivering in her trembling hands. "When he rode out here and told my pa he was gonna marry me, I told him in no uncertain terms to go to hell!"

"I know ya did," Dodge said. "I was right here where I am now—remember? But he gave you two weeks to ride to town on your own, or he was gonna send us, and he also said you weren't gonna like it if you forced his hand like that. I think it sort of embarrassed him—you not comin' in willin' like. He doesn't like how you're makin' him look in front of the whole town. So he sent us."

Dodge's voice dipped darkly. "He sent us, and, unfortunately, a whole passel of trouble. I'm sorry it's come to this. I truly am."

"This is crazy," Jennie said. "He can't force a girl to marry him. No man can. Not even Quentin Burnett!"

"Now, why don't you go on inside and pack a bag for yourself? You're comin' to town whether you want to or not. Whether it's *right* or not. You'd best get your family out of the house, as well, because me an' the boys here have been ordered to burn it to the ground. That's your punishment, see? I don't think you want them in there when we put the torch to it."

Jennie's heart kicked like a mule in her chest.

She loudly cocked the Sharps, hardened her jaws, and shook her long dark-brown hair back away from her cheeks. "You go to hell, you son of a bitch. I may not be able to get all of you, but I can get you, Dodge. If you take one step toward this cabin, I'll blow you out of your saddle!"

Dodge's face turned red with anger. "Did you hear a word I just said?"

Jennie did not respond to that. She aimed down the Sharps's barrel at Dodge. The other men were grinning now. The Miller brothers chuckled and looked at each other. Delvin Miller ducked his head and turned it to one side—a nervous twitch of sorts—while his brother, C.P., squirmed around lustily in his saddle.

"Go on inside and pack a bag," Dodge commanded, raising his voice. "Tell your family to evacuate the premises. This ranch now belongs to Mr. Quentin Burnett, as you yourself do, Miss Broyles. We mean your family no harm, but we have our orders." He rose slightly in his saddle as he raised his voice even louder. "Now, vamoose, damnit—I ain't gonna tell you again!"

From upstairs in the cabin, Mercy cried, "Poppa, no!"

Hard thuds of someone tramping around up there hit the air.

"Unhand me, damnit!" came the angry voice of Angus Broyles.

"Poppa, you can't go down there!" Mercy screamed.

Jennie glanced at the cabin's open door behind her. "Pa, stay upstairs!"

She returned her nervous gaze to Dodge. The gunman pointed a finger at her in warning. "If that old man comes out here with a gun, he's dead."

As if to demonstrate he meant what he'd said, Dodge shucked one of his Colts from its holster, and clicked the hammer back.

Jennie turned back to the cabin's open door. Mercy and Jacob were both yelling at their father now. Angus Broyles was coming down the stairs. He wore only his pajamas, a ratty blue robe open at the waist, and gray socks. His long, thin, tangled gray hair danced about his shoulders. His blue eyes were wild.

He clutched in both hands the old Colt Navy he'd used in the war and which he'd converted to metallic cartridges afterwards. He kept the weapon in a drawer of his nightstand.

"Pa, goddamnit!" Jennie ran back into the cabin. She set the Sharps on the table and raced to meet her father, grabbing his arm and trying to stop his progression toward the stoop. "They'll kill you, you old fool. You're not going out there with that gun!"

Mercy and Jacob stood on the stairs, Jacob near the top, Mercy in the middle. They were both yelling at their father.

"Unhand me, daughter!" Angus Broyles shouted, red-faced with fury. "No one is kidnapping my daughter or burning my cabin!"

"*Pa!*"

Jennie grabbed her father's arm once more. But the tall, stoop-shouldered sixty-three-year-old man was still strong despite the heart stroke he'd suffered a week ago and which had likely been caused in no small part by Burnett's demand for Jennie's hand in marriage.

He violently jerked his arm from Jennie's grip. The

force of the pull sent Jennie sprawling over a kitchen chair. She and the chair went down. Her head slammed hard against the floor puncheons.

"Poppa," she cried, trying to push herself up off the floor, her head swimming. She watched in horror as her father hurried around the table to the open door, holding the old Colt in his arthritic right hand, his thumb on the hammer.

As Angus Broyles walked through the doorway onto the stoop, he shouted, "Dodge, you tell Burnett he can take a fast ride down a steep—!"

A gun barked in the yard, cutting Broyles abruptly off.

Jennie swung a horrified look at the doorway. Her father had stopped in his tracks. Now he just stood there, unmoving. His right hand fell against his side. It opened. The Colt thumped to the floor.

There was another pistol blast in the yard.

Angus Broyles gasped and stumbled backward.

Another blast.

Another... and another... and Jennie watched in horror as blood spewed from the holes opening in her father's broad back as the bullets tore through his body, knocking him backwards into the cabin.

There were two more blasts, and then Angus Broyles twisted around with a ragged sigh and hit the kitchen floor, belly down, near Jennie with a thunderous boom.

"*Poppa*!" Jennie screamed.

Mercy and Jacob were screaming and bawling now, as well. Mercy ran down the stairs.

Jennie pushed up onto her hands and knees and crawled over to her father. Angus Broyles turned his big, gray head toward her. He opened his mouth to speak, but only blood oozed out from between his lips to flow over the warts on his chin.

He looked at his daughter, his eyes bright with shock.

"Pa!" Jennie sobbed.

Then Mercy and Jacob were down on their hands and knees beside her, screaming and bawling and leaning down to hug their dying father. The light left Angus Broyles's washed-out blue eyes, and his body trembled as life left him.

Outside, men were laughing.

Fury roared like a tidal wave through Jennie.

She shrugged off her dizziness from the fall, heaved herself to her feet, and grabbed the Sharps off the table. She cocked the rifle loudly as she stepped onto the porch.

"Goddamn you sons o'bitches!" she screamed as she raised the rifle to her shoulder, aiming into the yard.

But just as she saw that Vance Dodge was no longer where she'd last seen him, the man gave a chuckle and stepped up on her right. He grabbed the rifle. Jennie's finger snagged the trigger. The Sharps thundered.

Jennie screamed in rage as Dodge ripped the rifle from her hands.

She cursed again as she tried to punch Dodge, but he merely grabbed her wrist, twisted her around, and pushed her down the porch steps. She fell in the yard at the feet of the other men.

"Hold her while we fire the cabin," Dodge ordered as Mercy and Jacob continued to yell and bawl over their father's body.

"I'll do it," said C.P. Miller. "Not a problem. I'd call it a rare treat to hold Miss Jennie!"

As Jennie tried to climb to her feet, Miller grabbed her from behind and lifted her back off her feet. She was Miller's height, her head even with his. He kissed her cheek.

"Go fuck yourself, you limp-dicked little weasel!"

"What a tongue you got on you, girl!" Miller cried. "My dick ain't limp. Wanna see?"

His brother, Delvin, laughed.

Jennie reached for one of C.P.'s holstered pistols. Miller pulled the pistol out of her hand, stuffed it back down into its holster, and then grabbed both her arms, holding her as she struggled against him.

Meanwhile, Dodge stepped into the cabin, yelling, "You two get on outside less'n you wanna roast alive in here with that old rascal. Go on, now. Go on—*git!*"

Mercy was bawling hysterically. So was Jacob. They were both calling for their dead father.

"You can't!" Jennie screamed, still writhing against C.P. Miller. His brother was right there, too, laughing and pawing at Jennie's breasts with one hand, at her crotch with his other, while his brother held her from behind. "You can't burn us out! You bastards got no right!"

But then the Millers dragged Jennie back off toward the corral, a good distance from the cabin. They slammed her to the ground.

Holding her face down, one cheek mashed into the dirt and ground horseshit, both men pawed her now—grabbing her breasts and her bottom, running their hands up her skirt to brusquely caress her legs with their gloved hands.

One of them managed to stick a thick finger inside her.

"*Gahh!*" Jennie cried at the violation, squeezing her eyes closed against the raking pain.

A hand grabbed at her pantaloons. The pantaloons were being ripped down her legs.

"Let her go!"

It was Jacob's voice. Jennie opened her eyes to see her

brother run, stumbling toward her, holding his arms out in front of him, swinging his hands as though searching for something or someone to grab.

Delvin Miller rose from where he'd been nuzzling Jennie's neck and punched Jacob in the face. Jacob wheeled and hit the ground in a shuddering pile.

"No!" Mercy cried as, running out of the cabin, she saw the blind boy on the ground.

C.P. Miller was squirming around on Jennie's backside. "See there, now?" he yelled, laughing. "That dick ain't one bit limp!"

He pressed it into the crack between Jennie's buttocks.

"Is it, you little bitch?"

As he tried to force the head of his dick into her anus, Jennie gave a guttural, bellowing cry, twisted partway around, and raked her fingernails down C.P.'s face, drawing a bloody line starting from just above his right eye to his jawline. It was a deep, ragged, bloody gash.

Miller screamed girlishly, clutching his face with both hands. His pale, erect shaft bobbed up against his belly.

"Why, you little bitch!" barked Delvin Miller, glaring down at her.

He began unbuttoning his own fly.

"You're gonna choke on this, you little whore!"

His back was to the cabin now, from which smoke billowed. There was the crackling of oxygen-fed flames. Dodge and the other men walked up behind Delvin Miller. Miller couldn't hear their footsteps for the roaring of the flames.

Just as Miller pulled his erect manhood out of his fly, grinning proudly as he wagged it at Jennie, Dodge grabbed him from behind, spun him around, and punched him the face.

Miller screamed and stumbled backward. He tripped over Jennie and fell just beyond her, near where C.P. knelt, clutching his face in his hands.

"Burnett don't want her soiled, you damn fool!" Dodge railed, pointing an accusing finger at Delvin Miller. "That there is his wife—you understand? You're messin' with Burnett's *wife*, now! You think he'd appreciate one of you back-alley curs stickin' his filthy dick in her?"

Snarling like an enraged bobcat, Delvin Miller reached for one of his holstered pistols. Dodge stepped forward and kicked it out of his hand.

"Ow!" Delvin cried, grabbing his right wrist. "You bastard!"

"You try anything like that again, Miller," Dodge shouted, "I'll blow your head off. I'm Burnett's first lieutenant—you understand?" He punched his right index finger against Miller's chest. "That's me. I am. When Burnett's not around, I'm in charge. And right now I'm about that far from givin' you two dumbasses your walkin' papers."

He held up his thumb and index finger with a half an inch gap between them.

Delvin just stared at him. C.P. Miller pulled his hands away from his bloody face to glare down at Jennie. Blood dribbled from above his brow into the corner of his right eye. That eye was still in its socket, Jennie was sorry to see. She'd wanted to pluck it out.

She turned away from C.P. Miller to look at the cabin. She sobbed when she saw the smoke billowing out the cabin's windows. Her father had built the cabin with his own hands, with the help of his three children and their now-deceased mother. Now that cabin burned around the body of old Angus Broyles, whose gray-stockinged feet stuck out the front door, the toes facing downward.

The rest of his body was hidden by thickly churning gray smoke.

Jennie turned to where Mercy knelt beside their brother. Jacob sat with his legs stretched out before him. Blood trickled from his split lips. He appeared to be staring at the cabin, his round face drawn and pale with shock.

Mercy knelt beside him, grabbing at the ground and sobbing as she watched the cabin burn.

Dodge turned to Antelope Warner. "Well, ain't this been fun?" He jerked his head at Jennie. "I want her on my horse. Set her up there. Haze all them horses out of the corral, and let's get the hell out of here."

"What about those two, Vance?" asked Frank Sunday, glancing at Mercy and Jacob.

"Leave 'em," Dodge said. "They're scrubs. If they survive out here on their own, maybe we'll round 'em up with the rest of the scrubs in the fall gather."

Dodge swatted his hat against his thigh as he headed for his horse.

CHAPTER 3

"DODGE, LOOK!"

Vance Dodge turned to where Chick Holt was galloping off Dodge's right stirrup. Holt tossed his head to indicate a horseback rider sitting at the edge of a line of trees west of the trail, facing the galloping gang.

Dodge stopped his horse at the head of the pack, and the other riders followed suit. Jennie, riding behind Dodge, on Dodge's horse, with her hands cuffed around her kidnapper's waist to further humiliate her, cast her own gaze toward where Holt had indicated.

A man wearing a low-crowned, flat-brimmed black hat sat a mouse-colored horse at the edge of the pine forest spilling down from the western ridge, about a hundred yards away. Horse and rider sat seemingly staring toward Dodge's men, the horse idly switching its dark tail. Jennie recognized the man's longish dark-brown hair and the dark mustache folding down over his mouth. He was tall and broad, with thick shoulders.

Jennie also recognized the handsome, broad-barreled grullo the man straddled.

The man was George Hollis, a severe-looking, green-eyed man in his early thirties, possibly with some Indian blood—a relative newcomer to the mountains who'd taken over the claim of old Warren Van Hootin, a prospector, about four miles north of the Broyles place. Van Hootin had recently succumbed to a long illness, probably cancer.

A couple of months ago, Mr. Hollis had stopped by the Broyles cabin to introduce himself. He'd been polite and friendly, but there was something sad and brooding in him; his striking jade eyes set against the Indian russet of his chiseled face had seemed to be staring at something far away. He'd said nothing about himself except that he hailed from Nebraska, where the Broyles themselves were from, and that Van Hootin, a friend, had turned his claim over to him.

His reserved demeanor and the two big pistols he carried in addition to the Henry rifle in his saddle boot had told Jennie he might be a gunman. One who was on the run from the law.

She had never suspected he was one of Burnett's men. He carried himself with a singular, solitary air. Oddly, he'd seemed at once menacing and comforting, as though when a woman was in the presence of such a man, he would protect her at all costs. You did not, however, want to tangle with him.

He was alone, and there was something about him that said he would always be alone... forever and ever... in this life and beyond...

Now Jennie's heart fluttered in fear for the man. He was only one man, after all. If these seven men knew that he, too, had nested on range Quentin Burnett considered his own...

Just ride away, a voice inside her head urged the solitary stranger. Just ride away. There's nothing you can do here except get yourself killed. Even if you're good with your guns, you're outnumbered by some of the savviest killers on the frontier.

"Who the hell is that?" Dodge asked no one in particular.

"Hell if I know," said Holt.

"Another nester, most like." Antelope Warren spat distastefully to one side. "They're gettin' thick as goddamn rats in these mountains."

Dodge shuttled his gaze from where Hollis sat staring at him, at where the smoke from the cabin unspooled against the sky. The cabin was too far away to see, but the smoke was clear. Jennie knew what Dodge was thinking.

The stranger had seen the smoke and was on his way to investigate.

Jennie's heart thudded.

"Maybe it's time to do a little more herd-thinnin'." Dodge turned to the Miller brothers. "Why don't you two make yourselves useful for a change?" He canted his head toward the rider on the mouse-brown horse. He said nothing more.

The Millers' cold grins meant they understood what they'd been ordered to do.

"No!" Jennie blurted. "You've done enough killing here today, Dodge. Leave him alone!"

Dodge craned his neck sharply to scowl at his prisoner. "Who is that?"

"I don't know," Jennie said. "He's probably just drifting through. No more killing, Dodge. *Please.* All right?"

Dodge studied her darkly, then smiled just as darkly, his gaze dropping to her breasts. "You're even purtier when you're beggin'—you know that? If you wasn't Burnett's woman, I'd ask you what you'd do in exchange for leavin' that fella alone. But Burnett's done staked his claim on you, gallblastit."

He looked at the Millers.

"No!" Jennie pleaded.

"No problem," said C.P. Miller, glaring at Jennie.

Jennie stared in dread as the two Millers galloped off toward the dark stranger, who continued to sit the grullo, facing them, almost as though he were waiting for them. Beckoning them, even...

Ride away, Jennie silently urged him. Just ride away!

"Let's get movin'!" Dodge called to the others.

They moved out. Jennie glanced back over her shoulder as the Millers approached Mr. Hollis, who continued to sit his horse, facing them.

He had no idea what he was in for.

Jesse James had walked away from a fight with the Millers.

Ten minutes later, two shots rang out, the second one on the heels of the first. Their echoes rolled skyward, dwindling gradually.

Jennie jerked with a start, as though the bullets had been meant for her. She stared straight ahead. She felt like sobbing, but she was all sobbed out.

Dodge glanced at Chick Holt riding beside him. The men shared brief, satisfied smiles.

———

GIDEON HAWK UNSNAPPED THE KEEPER THONG FROM over the hammer of the big, top-break Russian .44 holstered for the cross-draw on his left hip. Then he unsnapped the keeper thong from over the Colt Peacemaker thonged on his right thigh, which was clad in black whipcord.

He sat straight-backed, grim-faced in his saddle,

watching the two riders gallop toward him, their horses sort of hop-skipping over the low, spidery wolf willows. As the men drew nearer, their horses snorting, Hawk saw that the pair shared familial features—namely, pinched-up, stupid, mean-looking eyes and weak chins. One had dark-brown hair while the other was sandy-headed and taller.

The smaller, darker rider had a nasty fresh gash down the right side of his face.

He'd been scratched. Badly scratched... no doubt by a girl fighting him.

Likely, the same girl whom Hawk had seen riding on the back of the horse of the gang's lead rider and who'd turned her head to stare in his direction until she and the rest of the gang had galloped out of sight.

The riders—both in their early twenties and filled to their tinhorn brims with piss and rattlesnake venom—pulled back on their reins, stopping their horses about fifty feet away from Gideon Henry Hawk.

The two firebrands sat for a time, keeping their horses' heads raised, studying the dark stranger while he stared back at them, his calm expression belying the anxiety he felt for the fate of the girl the gang had taken away.

The girl he'd met once a few weeks ago and whose name, he remembered, was Jennie.

Jennie Broyles.

You didn't find many girls like her in this remote place. You didn't find many girls like her anywhere. He remembered her because you didn't forget girls like her—beautiful in an offhand, unconscious way, and with a spirited, devilish light dancing like sunlit diamonds in her brown eyes. Those eyes and the light, effortless way she'd moved had reminded Hawk of his dead wife, Linda.

That would be her cabin burning to the east. Hawk had ridden down from his own mountain shack to investigate the smoke, though he'd known that by the time he reached the cabin, it would be too late for him to do anything about the fire.

"What the hell you lookin' at?" asked the dark young man with the bloody scratch on his face.

"I'm lookin' at you," Hawk said. "And you're lookin' at me. Now that we got that important ground covered, who the hell are you and where are you taking the young lady? *Against her will.*"

"What the hell is that to you?" asked the taller, sandy-haired rider, slitting his eyes beneath his hat brim upon which the sun laid a thin pool of glowing salmon light. The sun shone copper in his muddy brown eyes.

"Oh, I don't know. I reckon it's up to any man to be concerned when a girl is being hauled away from her burning cabin... obviously against her will."

"Why, you plug-headed fool," said the shorter, darker brother. "Don't you know it ain't healthy for folks not to mind their own business? What's your name?"

"Gideon Hawk." He'd been going by the name of George Hollis to avoid trouble, for he had a sizable bounty on his head. But it didn't matter if these two knew his real name. He doubted they'd be alive much longer.

"You live around here, Hawk?"

"I do."

"Where?"

"I took over the Van Hootin claim."

The two brothers glanced at each other, then turned back to Hawk.

"Now, why in hell would you do a fool thing like that?" asked the darker of the two.

"I reckon I didn't see it as a fool thing."

The darker brother gave a caustic snort, as though he were dealing with a hoopleheaded tinhorn. "This land belongs to one Mr. Quentin Burnett, you damn fool. He's about the biggest stick in the woods around here. And he don't like nesters. There's already enough nesters on Burnett's range the way it is, and if you think he's gonna sit still while another one gets himself all burrowed in, you got another think comin'."

The sandy-haired brother said, "Especially one so nosy."

"And especially a half-breed," added the darker brother. "You might wear the clothes of a white man, but you're just as Injun as Geronimo, as far as any *white* man is concerned. Shit!"

"Maybe I better go down and talk to this big stick myself," Hawk said. "If Burnett thinks he owns this range, he's got it wrong. Maybe someone better set him straight before he brings a passel of trouble down on himself and earns himself a wooden overcoat."

The darker brother laughed. "Who's gonna earn him that overcoat? *You?*"

Hawk blinked slowly.

"Well, now, ain't that—!"

"Hey, C.P.," interrupted the lighter brother.

"What?"

The sandy-haired brother was staring somewhat incredulously at Hawk. He opened his mouth a full ten seconds before he spoke. "I think... I think I seen this fella's face on a handbill... time or two before."

"Wouldn't doubt it a bit, Del," said C.P., hiking a shoulder. "Reckon he don't wear them big pistols 'cause he thinks they look purty on his person. Doubt he's a man of the Lord. But that don't mean—"

"Gideon Hawk," Del said, his voice pitched with awe. "The rogue lawman."

C.P. stared appraisingly at Hawk, his gaze raking the big, green-eyed man up and down—from the crown of his black hat down past his black, wool-lined vest and blue plaid shirt to his guns to the cuffs of his whipcord trousers shoved into the mule-eared tops of his low-heeled cavalry boots.

C.P. returned his gaze to Hawk's eyes now. C.P. looked edgy. Deep lines cut into the skin above the bridge of his nose. He watched in silent horror as a grim smile began to pull very slowly at the corners of Gideon Hawk's broad mouth, beneath the dark-brown mustache curving down around it.

Del stared at Hawk, as well. Both young men looked like two boys who had been poking a stick at a snake only to just now discover said snake was poisonous and as mean as the meanest demon-viper in the bowels of the devil's own hell.

Del's eyes snapped wide as he reached for one of his pistols, shouting, "Let's take him, C.P.!"

He didn't get his revolver even half out of its leather before Hawk jerked up the Russian and blew C.P. out of his saddle.

C.P. had not yet disappeared, rolling backward off the rear end of his coyote dun, before Del joined him in the same violent manner, blood lapping from the .44-caliber-sized hole in his chest. Del triggered his own Smith & Wesson wild just before he hit the ground with a crunching thud.

Hawk held his grullo's reins taut in his left hand as his victims' two mounts whinnied, wheeled, and ran off in the direction from which they'd come, their bridle reins bouncing over the wolf willows. Hawk looked at the pair of doomed shooters.

Del lay the farthest away from Hawk, on his side, his back facing his killer.

He lay sort of curled up, arms crossed on his chest, shivering.

C.P. lay a little nearer, belly up. He stared up at the sky, spread-eagled, in glassy-eyed shock. He flapped his arms and legs as though he were trying to become airborne.

"Oh," he said, flopping his arms and legs again as frothy blood spilled from the hole in his upper right chest. "Oh, shit..." He lifted his head with effort and looked at the hole, then let his head flop back down against the ground. "Lung shot!"

Hawk swung down from the grullo's back. Holding his Russian straight down along his right leg, he walked over and stood staring down at C.P., who stared up at him, moving his lips and making gurgling sounds in his throat.

"Oh, shit," C.P. said. Raw horror widened his eyes. "I... I can't die! I've done bad things! I can't die! I can't go there! Please... help me!"

This last came out in a voice pinched with sorrow mixed with terror. Tears oozed from his eyes. "I can't die! I can't die, ya see, Mr. Hawk!"

"You've come to that realization a mite late in the game, boy," Hawk said, aiming his Russian at C.P. He cocked the pistol and narrowed one eye as he stared down the barrel. "Where are they taking the girl?"

"Wha... huh?"

"Where are they taking the girl?"

C.P.'s lips were quivering in horror. Then his eyes turned mean and defiant. He tried to spit at Hawk, but only bloody saliva dribbled over his lower lip. "You got to hell," he said in a phlegmy voice. "Fuck you! You done killed me! Fuck you!"

Hawk slid the Russian lower on C.P.'s body. He aimed at C.P.'s right knee. He blew a hole through it.

C.P. screamed and convulsed, flopping madly in place.

Hawk aimed at his other knee.

"No!" C.P. screamed shrilly. "They're takin' her to Burnett. In New Canaan! Taking her to Burnett for marryin'!"

Hawk frowned at C.P., who was shuddering and sobbing now, quivering on the ground as though he were being struck over and over by lightning.

"What did you say? *Marryin'*..."

"Burnett's gonna marry that wildcat! Oh, Christ... I'm in pain here... and I'm gonna die and swim forever more in a burnin' lake of liquid fire!"

"Yes, you are." Hawk aimed the Russian at C.P.'s head. C.P. stared up at him, his eyes crossing and widening as he realized what was about to happen. He raised his hands as though to shield his face from the bullet. Hawk fired through the shooter's right hand and into his forehead.

C.P.'s arms flopped to the ground for the last time.

"Time you shut up about it," Hawk said. "I'm tired of listening to such nonsense. A boy like you was born to burn in hell." He turned to Del.

Hawk walked over and saw that Del was still breathing, though he wasn't moving much. Del looked up at him in exasperation. "You're faster'n us? No one's faster'n us, goddamnit."

"Ain't that the way it goes?" Hawk said, clicking the Russian's hammer back. "You never know when and from which direction it's gonna come. It's always a surprise. No more surprises for you, my friend."

"Ah, hell," Del said, staring at the Russian bearing down on him.

Hawk shot Del through the kid's left eye, then holstered the smoking Russian. He stood staring along the trail to New Canaan for a time, planning his next course of action.

He turned to where the smoke from the Broyles cabin continued to furl up beyond the pines. The old man would be there. And the blind boy and the little girl. What was her name?

Mercy?

Hawk would help them first. If there was anything left to help, that was.

Then he'd see to their sister.

"Odd way to ask for a girl's hand," Hawk muttered as he swung up onto the grullo's back and galloped toward the cabin.

CHAPTER 4

THE TOWN OF NEW CANAAN SAT IN A LUSH VALLEY surrounded by jagged mountain peaks still streaked with snow even this late in the summer.

The valley was like the setting for a jewel, and the town of New Canaan was the jewel. But only if said jewel was about the unloveliest chunk of rock a poor, raggedy-heeled groom could get his hands on.

The valley was a large slice of heaven complete with an alpine stream wending its way down its middle. The town was a smoky fetid hell, a collection of motley log shacks and tumbledown rail corrals and privies and trash heaps and scorched tents and whores' cribs scattered willy-nilly around the business district.

In nearly every muddy alley you could find a man or even a woman sleeping off a long bender. Maybe a cur or two sniffing at them to see if they were a viable food source.

One or two of those men or women might be dead from a knife in the belly or a bullet in the back, and a cur or a wolf that had sneaked in from the mountains might be trying to tear a limb off.

The crown jewel of the business district was the New Canaan Inn owned by Quentin Burnett. Named after Mount Canaan, the tallest peak in the chain of mountains surrounding the town, the New Canaan Inn appeared about as out of place here as would a princess in white gloves and a satin gown. It was the one building in New Canaan that would have looked right at home in the heart of Denver or Dodge City or Tombstone or even Leadville.

The ambitious structure was sprawling and gaudy, with ornate painted scrollwork and with balconies off all three floors. A large sign announcing itself stretched across the top of the third story. The sign was so large, it could be read by riders—any rider who could read, that was (and those were damn few in this remote section of Idaho)—riding down out of the mountains looking for a bowl of elk stew, a mattress dance with a cheap whore, and a bottle of busthead to ease the aches and pains that were part and parcel of ranching or prospecting or running trap lines or capturing and breaking wild horses, which were the primary means of sustainment in this neck of the frontier outback.

The legitimate means, that was. There was plenty of outlawry, as well.

Jennie had taught herself to read, if only rudimentarily so, so she'd been able to read the NEW CANAAN INN sign as she'd ridden down out of the mountains, her hands cuffed around Vance Dodge. The light was failing, but a few stray rays of the setting sun glittered upon the sign as though to mock the captive girl.

The sign had made her sick. But she didn't let on. She kept her expression stoic. On the ride down out of the mountains, leaving her burning cabin and dead father and bereaved siblings behind her, she'd tried very hard to turn her mind to stone.

The only thought she allowed in was that of sticking a knife or anything else sharp into the belly of the man who'd murdered her father, burned her out, and kidnapped her to rape her. That's essentially what Burnett's plan was. He called it marriage. It was rape.

A knife, Jennie thought as she and the gang members rode into town. *I have to get my hands on a knife.*

As Dodge, Jennie, and the rest of Burnett's men entered the heart of the fetid business district, the tents, log cabins, and stock corrals giving way to a few false-fronted buildings including the New Canaan, one of the men at the rear of the pack called, "Hey, Dodge!"

Dodge stopped and turned his horse with a sigh. "What is it this time, Sunday?"

Frank Sunday canted his head to indicate the two horses galloping toward them. Both wore saddles but no riders. Their bridle reins trailed along the ground behind them.

"What in Sam Hill...?" Dodge said.

Chick Holt booted his own horse back toward the two riderless horses, both of which stopped near the group's rear and stood blowing and shaking their heads. They were sweat-lathered and owl-eyed. They'd galloped far and hard to catch up to the gang.

Jennie could tell they were also frightened. She'd seen similar looks in her own horses' eyes after violent mountain thunderstorms.

Holt rode around both horses, scrutinizing them closely, and then galloped back up to Dodge, scowling with incredulity.

"Them's the Miller boys' hosses," he said. "There's blood on their saddles."

Dodge blinked dully, uncomprehendingly. "Shit, you say!"

"There's blood on both saddles, all right," said Frank Sunday, who was now scrutinizing the horses himself. He looked toward Dodge, brows furled with befuddlement. "Satan himself couldn't have outgunned those two hog-wallopin' sons of bitches!"

Jennie looked back at the steep ridge they'd just ridden down. Despite the stone she'd tried to turn herself into, as she stared at those forest-clad, snow-mantled peaks behind her, she felt a faint smile pull weakly at the corners of her mouth.

Dodge stared at the horses. He looked off toward the ridge, as though he half-expected to see the Millers walking down out of the mountains. Then, obviously unable to fathom what had caused the Millers' horses to be missing their riders, he gave a disgruntled snort, swung his own horse around, and booted it on up the street.

New Canaan was bustling with early evening foot and horse traffic. Shadows were lengthening and the lamps in windows on both sides of the street were brightening. Piano and fiddle music emanated from several saloons. Judging by the boisterous male laughter also coming from those saloons and from the town's several brothels, men had come down out of the mountains to stomp with their tails up.

Smoke from chimneys and cookfires hung thick in the air. That and the stench from overfilled latrines set Jennie's eyes to watering.

Dodge pulled his horse up in front of the New Canaan. Jennie's heart skipped several beats when she saw Quentin Burnett himself sitting on the broad front porch with several other men in similar fancy attire, complete with bowler hats and polished boots.

Burnett and the others were smoking large cigars and drinking liquor from fancy glasses.

One of Burnett's brethren had a girl straddling his knee —obviously a working girl, for she displayed more skin than flimsy gown, and green and pink feathers danced in her hair.

"Mr. Burnett," Dodge called.

Burnett was so absorbed in conversation with the other men that he hadn't heard Dodge or seen his riders ride up. Finally, when Dodge called again, louder, Burnett stopped talking and turned to him, as did the other men around him as well as the whore, who slid a strap of her skimpy dress up onto her shoulder, covering her breasts.

The man whose knee she was sitting on, facing him, had been playing with the girls breasts and laughing seedily.

Burnett scowled, peeved at the interruption. Then, seeing the group of gunslingers on the street before him, he arched his eyebrows expectantly, and rose from his chair—a big, portly man in his late fifties, with a beet-red face sandwiched by thick, curly muttonchop whiskers.

Small, round, steel-framed spectacles sat up high on his broad wedge of a nose. He squinted through the glasses, canting his head a little to one side to scrutinize the young woman riding behind Dodge.

"Ahh, there she is," said Burnett through his large, white, false teeth. "Gentlemen, the Queen of New Canaan has arrived!"

The eight or so other men sitting with Burnett all rose with interest, including the gent who'd been holding the whore. He'd risen so quickly that the whore had plopped to her butt on the porch floor with a clipped yowl. The girl quickly regained her feet and dashed off, barefoot and indignant, into the saloon.

The men, most of whom appeared around Burnett's age—late fifties, early sixties—muttered amongst themselves as they cast their pointed gazes toward Jennie, still sitting behind Dodge, her arms wrapped around his waist. Burnett clutched the lapels of his long, green wool coat as he made his way down the porch steps. His hat and coat were green while his vest and pants were brown, his shirt white, his tie black.

As he approached, Jennie felt her insides shrivel.

Burnett came over to stand beside Dodge's horse, smiling up at Jennie. His eyes were large and blue behind the spectacles. They raked Jennie up and down.

"She'll do," Burnett said, grinning. "Oh, she'll do very well indeed." He leveled his gaze on Jennie herself. "I've admired you from afar, young lady. When I saw you in town with your father, I knew I had to have you. You're mine now. You might as well get used to it. In time, you're even going to enjoy it. I'll lavish you with gifts!"

Jennie worked up a mouthful of saliva, leaned out away from Dodge's horse, and spat in Burnett's face. Part of the spray splattered his glasses.

Burnett jerked backwards, closing his eyes, shaking his head, and removing his spectacles from his nose.

The men on the porch gasped and muttered their reproof.

"Why, you little—!" Dodge said, snapping an angry look at Jennie.

"No, no," Burnett said, holding a hand up.

He raised his glasses, and, grinning, turned to the men standing on the porch. He drew the glasses close to his face, stuck out his fat little pink tongue, and licked the spittle off the right lens.

The men on the porch all laughed and clapped.

Fury exploded inside of Jennie, who leaned out again from the side of Dodge's horse, and shouted, "*Murderer*! You killed my father and burned our barn! When my neighbors learn about what happened, you can rest assured the U.S. marshals will be called in. You're going to hang, Burnett!"

"Oh," Burnett said, setting his glasses back down on his nose. "Do you think so?" He turned once more to the porch, and beckoned. "Henry, would you mind coming down here and introducing yourself to my lovely bride?"

The man on whose lap the whore had been sitting stepped away from his chair and descended the porch steps. He was of medium height, compact, lean and grain-haired, with a neat gray mustache. He wore a gray suit with a gray bowler hat. His eyes were small and steely, his deeply suntanned nose straight and long. His previous dalliance with the whore notwithstanding, he wore about him the righteous, intimidating air of a man of the cloth.

He came to stand beside Burnett, smiling up at Jennie. "Hello, Mrs. Burnett," he said, grinning. "I'm Henry Blackwell, Chief Marshal of the Northwestern Territories."

He slid his left lapel back to reveal the moon-and-star badge pinned to his vest.

Jennie felt her lower jaw sag in shock.

The men on the porch all laughed.

CHAPTER 5

HAWK GALLOPED ALONG THE MOUNTAIN TRAIL TOWARD where smoke from the burning Broyles cabin rose beyond a fringe of pines that were nearly black now in the deepening twilight. When the grullo galloped around a bend in the trail, the cabin appeared.

Or what was left of the cabin.

Mostly, there were only dark-gray smoke and orange flames. Cinders shone in the column of billowing smoke, winking like fireflies. The smoke rose high to fade against the darkening sky.

Hawk halted his horse just beyond the ranch portal and cast his gaze around the yard. He saw two people in the yard fronting the cabin, closer to the unpeeled pine rail corral, whose gate was drawn wide. The corral was empty.

One of the two people Hawk could see through the smoke was down on both knees, staring forlornly at the burning cabin. The other one—the Broyles boy, it appeared—was wandering in slow circles around the girl on the ground. Hawk could see that the girl was sobbing, her shoulders jerking.

Hawk booted the grullo ahead and steered it in a broad circle around the cabin and dancing cinders. The heat from the fire pressed hard against him, causing the darkening air to shiver. As he approached the girl and the boy, the girl jerked her head toward him suddenly and lurched to her feet, stumbling backward.

The boy had already stopped walking aimlessly. He faced Hawk, his blind eyes wide as though staring at Hawk, though he appeared to be blindly gazing a little beyond the newcomer. The boy tipped his head this way and that, listening.

"Who is it?" the boy called, his voice brittle with fear. "Who's there?"

"It's George Hollis," Hawk called, reining his horse to a stop before the girl, who stood staring up at him, her eyes glazed with shock. "I'm George Hollis, from the Van Hootin cabin. I stopped by a few weeks back." There was no point in confusing the boy and the girl about the alias.

Hawk swung down from the leather. The boy and the girl stood facing him, the girl continuing to weep, her face a tortured mask of bitter tears. The boy, too, had been crying, his eyes puffy, cheeks red and wet. Their cheeks were muddy with the soot from the fire.

"Poppa's inside," the girl sobbed, convulsing and turning to slowly lift her arm and point her index finger at the cabin. "Poppa's inside! He's inside!" She looked at Hawk, her body wracked with grief. "Can you help him?"

Hawk turned to the cabin. Part of the roof had already fallen in. Through the gaps in the burned-out walls and through the windows he could see that the inside of the cabin was like a fully stoked stove. Anyone inside was burned to a crisp.

"Christ," he said, feeling his heart twist in his chest. He walked heavily forward, dropping to a knee before the girl. "I don't think there's anything I can do for your pa, child. I'm sorry."

Hawk placed his hand on the girl's arm, and gently squeezed it.

Oh, such sorrow. Such bitter sorrow. When will it ever end?

"He's inside the cabin!" the girl cried.

"They killed him," the young man said. Hawk remembered that his name was Jacob. The little girl was Mercy. "They killed him and took our sister. It was Quentin Burnett, though Burnett wasn't here. It was Dodge. Dodge and six others."

"I know, boy," Hawk said. "I saw them ridin' off with your sister. Don't you worry about her. I'm gonna get her back for you."

Neither child reacted to what he'd said. If they'd been able to understand him, they'd likely not believed him. It was well known in these parts that no one messed with Quentin Burnett and lived to tell the tale.

These two young Broyles siblings were in shock, their minds numb. Hawk knew how they felt. He'd felt the same way when he'd seen his beloved child, Jubal Hawk, hanging from that cottonwood branch in a raging prairie rainstorm —the branch from which the vile "Three Fingers" Ned Meade had hung the boy to get even with Hawk's having brought Meade's child-killing brother to justice.

Hawk had felt that same overpowering fog of numbness when he'd found that his wife, Linda, had hung herself from the cottonwood tree in their backyard in Nebraska, out of her unbearable grief at Jubal's fate.

Hawk glanced around to see if any of the Broyles horses had lingered near. He didn't see any. Finally, he turned to the two Broyles children, and said, "I'm gonna get you two up to my cabin. It's not far. There's no point in your staying around here. You'll be safe there. I'll see to it."

"I don't... I don't wanna leave Poppa!" the girl cried.

"Mercy, there's nothing you can do for him now. Your poppa's gone. I have to get you out of here. And then I'm gonna get your sister back." Hawk rose and turned to the girl's brother. "Jacob, I'd like you to climb onto my horse. Will you do that?"

Young Broyles just stood looking around as though he were trying to get everything straight in his head. But Hawk knew he wouldn't be able to get anything that had happened here this night straight for a long time. Maybe he never would.

Hawk walked over and touched the boy's arm. Jacob flinched and pulled back, looking frightened. He was a strong, good-looking boy though his eyes were pale and a little off-putting. Hawk knew the boy was good with a skinning knife. The outside of the Broyles cabin had been decorated with skins and furs young Jacob had tanned.

"It's all right, Jacob. I know you don't want to leave here. But there's nothing for you here anymore. I'd like to take you up to my cabin. You and your sister can ride my horse and I'll walk. Okay? Can you understand what I'm telling you, son?"

Jacob drew a deep, ragged breath. He looked around. More tears slithered down his cheeks. They glistened orange in the firelight. He turned toward the cabin, and said, "I reckon . . . that'd be best. Mercy, come on, honey. We're gonna go with Mr. Hollis."

"Are you going, Jacob?" the girl asked.

"Yeah, I'm going. No point in staying here."

"What about Poppa?"

"He's gone, Mercy. We gotta think about getting Jennie back now."

Mercy was staring at the cabin. The fire was gradually losing its intensity. As another portion of the roof collapsed into the leaping flames, Mercy walked over to Hawk's horse.

She extended her hand to Hawk, and he lifted her up onto his saddle. She was so light, she seemed almost like nothing in his hands. For some reason, that gave his heart another twist and a pull.

Then he helped Jacob up into the leather, as well.

"Goodbye, Poppa," Mercy sobbed as Hawk began leading the grullo out through the ranch portal, the cabin's flames dying behind him, the mountain's dense, dark night tumbling down around him.

Hawk led the horse and its two riders wide around the two men he'd killed, and then found the mouth of the trail that wound up the side of the ridge toward his cabin nestled in the next valley.

The sky turned from green to black, but the stars were sharp at this altitude, offering enough light to keep Hawk on the tan strip of trail switchbacking up the ridge through the dark pines. As he walked, the horse clomping along behind him, Mercy broke into strings of intermittent sobs. The smoke from the Broyles's burning cabin occasionally touched his nose as the breeze blew up from the valley below.

When he was halfway up the ridge, Hawk stopped suddenly. The horse stopped behind, the bit rattling in its teeth. The horse gave an incredulous blow.

Hawk had heard something.

He stepped wide of the horse to stare along his back trail.

The short hairs bristled across the back of his neck.

"What is it?" Jacob said, his quiet, worried voice sounding loud in the quiet night. "Why are we stopping?"

"Shh," Hawk said. "Prob'ly nothin', but I'm gonna check it out just the same." He slid his sixteen-shot repeating Henry rifle from the scabbard strapped to his saddle.

"What is it, Mr. Hollis?" Mercy said, her voice trembling.

"I don't think it's anything at all, honey," Hawk said, placing a reassuring hand on the girl's thigh. "Probably just a deer or a nightbird or some-such. I'm gonna take a little walk back along our trail to be sure."

Hawk gave Mercy his horse's bridle reins. "You take these. Hold 'em loose. The grullo knows his way back to the cabin, and, it bein' past his suppertime, he'll likely head right there. When you get there, go on inside and make yourselves to home. Should be some lamps lit. You'll find a blond-headed woman there. That's my wife. My boy, Jubal, is there, too. Linda's likely fixin' supper. She'll make you feel right to home. I'll be along shortly."

"A blond-headed woman?" Mercy said.

"That'll be my wife. She's very accommodating. She'll make you feel right to home."

In his mind, Hawk was seeing his house back in Nebraska, not the little prospector's shack old Van Hootin had built at the bottom of the next valley, along a creek he'd named after himself and along which he had several gold diggings. Things were getting mixed up in Hawk's mind, though he didn't realize it. It was almost like he'd fallen half-asleep and was dreaming, reality infused with the smoke and shadows of fancy.

"Oh," Mercy said, uncertainly. She brushed the heel of her hand across her wet nose, sniffing. "All right."

Hawk slapped the grullo's rump, and the horse

thumped on up the trail. As the horse and its riders made the turn onto another switchback, Hawk heard Mercy faintly say to her brother, "I didn't even know Mr. Hollis was married…"

Hawk felt his mouth corners rise slightly at that, his belly filled with the warm feeling that thinking about his family always gave him. Now, holding the Henry in both hands across his chest, he made his way slowly down the trail. When he'd walked roughly ten yards, a vague shadow moved between two trees off the trail to his left.

"Hold it," Hawk said in a low voice, pulling back behind a near tree and sliding his gaze out around the side of it. "I saw you. Name yourself!"

No response.

In the far distance, a lone wolf howled.

Hawk held his position, heart quickening slightly as he awaited the blast of a rifle.

When none came, he slid another cautious glance out around the side of the fir tree. "Who are you? Name yourself." He paused, running his tongue along his bottom lip. "Luke?" He waited. "That you, Luke?"

Nothing.

Hawk said, "I told you, ole buddy, that if you tried to hunt me down, I'd kill you. Now, I don't want to do that, but you give me no choice."

A loud thud from maybe twenty yards downslope.

Hawk stepped out around the tree, racked a cartridge into the Henry's breech, and snapped the rifle's butt against his shoulder.

Another hard thud, and another.

Hawk began to squeeze the Henry' trigger but then eased the tension in his finger when he saw the silhouette of the deer bounding at a slant down the slope. The beast bounded straight up in the air again, lifting all four feet off the ground, to hurtle over a deadfall.

It landed with another thud as all four hooves hit the ground at the same time, and then disappeared over the shoulder of the slope.

Hawk lowered the Henry and scowled off down the ridge. He looked around, ears pricked.

"Luke?" he said quietly.

Why did he have this overwhelming feeling that the kid he'd taken under his wing, oh so long ago, Deputy U.S. Marshal Luke Morgan, was following him? The sense that Morgan was indeed on his trail was nonetheless powerful despite a vague region of Hawk's brain remembering that he'd killed the young lawman—by accident—several years ago.

He'd hoped Morgan would kill him, Hawk, and put him out of his infernal misery. But Hawk had been surprised to see the shooter bearing down on him, and, reacting instinctively, he'd shot the young lawman he'd only a few months before considered his understudy. His younger brother.

And whom he'd later hoped would be his executioner.

But Hawk had shot him dead.

Add another misery to Hawk's trail...

Still, a large, increasingly irrational portion of his conscious mind told him that Morgan was back there. Somewhere.

Dogging him...

Trying to stop his vigilante run, to stop him from wiping out evil across the frontier. He couldn't let that happen now. He'd become too good at this. Killing bad men had become his irrefutable, irresistible calling. Every man he killed was one more bell being tolled for his dead wife, his dead son.

He might have just now spooked a deer, not stumbled on Morgan. Still, Morgan was back there. Hawk knew he was, despite Morgan being dead. That's the way Hawk's brain was working these days. Or not working. Chief Marshal Henry Clay had sent Morgan. The younker was lying back, waiting for his chance to snuff Hawk's wick.

Hawk looked around again slowly, carefully. His hearing had become so keen that he thought he could hear aphids growing on distant tree limbs. Sometimes he thought he could hear the ocean waves lapping upon a distant shore, or the muffled roar of a fire igniting a distant star.

But hearing nothing nearby now that could be construed as a human stalker, Hawk shouldered his rifle and continued on up the slope. Linda would likely have the coffee pot on the range, waiting for him.

Jubal would likely be sitting at the table, waiting for supper to be served, carving another wooden horse he loved so much to carve, putting his folding Barlow knife down occasionally to gallop the lifelike horse along the edge of the table, making galloping sounds with his lips.

Another bucking bronco.

Hawk smiled, adjusted the angle of his hat, and increased his pace. He had to get home to his family.

CHAPTER 6

JENNIE BROYLES HAD SAT SO LONG IN THE BATHTUB, the water had gone cold. For the past hour or so, she'd been sitting in the cooling water, staring out the tiny window at the peak of the gable ten feet above her, in a large, unfinished attic room of the New Canaan Inn.

Hearing the raucous voices in the street below the room, and smelling the woodsmoke from the town's many fires, Jennie gave a shiver. She looked down at the water.

The bubbles from the scented lye soap she'd been given had disappeared. The water had turned the color of cast iron. Her knees, which she hugged against her breasts, had turned fish-belly white and were as wrinkled as any old woman's.

"You need a hand out of there?" Dixie asked from where she lounged on the red velvet fainting couch behind Jennie.

Dixie was the woman whom Burnett had ordered Dodge to turn Jennie over to for tending. By "tending," he'd obviously meant locking her up in the sparsely furnished attic room that functioned as a bedroom, and forcing her to take a bath.

Two other whores had filled the tub and scrubbed Jennie down with brushes and sponges. They'd washed her hair and held her head underwater longer than necessary, rinsing her. She'd heard them chuckling while she'd held her breath and felt the pressure build in her head.

When Jennie was what they'd deemed clean, despite one saying, "There was no getting the cow shit out of a ranch girl's hide," they'd left, leaving only Dixie in the room.

Dixie was obviously a soiled dove. A whore. Judging by the lines around her mouth and eyes, she was considerably older than Jennie and the two other whores who'd bathed her against her will. Dixie had obviously been pretty once, for she sported a delicately boned, evenly featured face and long, dark-red hair that hung in rivulets about her shoulders. The hair had been dyed, Jennie suspected.

Dixie lounged back on the settee now, both feet on the floor. Her body was angled to one side, and she rested her cheek on the heel of her fine-boned hand. She wore pantaloons and a chemise over a corset, and high-heeled, black boots with silver buckles. On each wrist, she wore a ruffled black garter. Her hair was held back from her forehead with a tightly wound black bandanna, the long tail of which fell down the back of her head before curling forward to hang down over her right shoulder, nearly to her lap.

Her lips were thin. Too thin for her, even in her young days, to have had what anyone would have called a pretty mouth. Her nose was short and upturned. She was pale, attesting to her not getting much sunlight. But then, most of the whores Jennie had seen on her forced march to the attic had been as pale as ghosts—except for the black girl and the several Mexicans she'd seen, of course.

Jennie turned to her. "How long are you gonna sit there?"

"For as long as it takes."

"For as long as what takes?"

"For as long as it takes for you to submit to him —Quentin."

Jennie chuffed with exasperation. "I'm never gonna submit to him. You'll die of old age, sitting right there."

"You will eventually. You'll have to. You'll go stir crazy up here. Finally, you'll realize you're better off submitting to Quentin than being locked in this room, whiling away the days. They all do... eventually."

"They *all* do? How many have there been?"

"Quentin's wives? There were four before you."

"I am not, nor will I ever be, Burnett's wife."

"All right, then," Dixie said. "He's had four wives up till *now*. There, is that better?"

"What happened to them?"

"Let me see," Dixie said, leaning forward, resting her elbows on her knees, and tapping fingers against her chin. "The first was a traditional marriage that came to an end a long, long time ago. The marriage happened before Quentin got rich. I never knew the lady. Have no idea how she ended up. Don't really want to know. The second was me."

"You."

"Me. And, you see, I got old. At least too old for Burnett. I'm thirty-three. He likes them your age... forever and ever. So he kicked me out of his chamber and married a girl called Sweetheart. A gold miner's daughter. Sweetheart submitted right away. In fact, Sweetheart and her family thought it was the best thing in the world for the girl.

"Sweetheart was the queen of the third floor, which is Burnett's own private residence. Only problem was Sweetheart went soft in the head after she had a child, and ran away. Burnett had her tracked down. What happened to her is anyone's guess, but if I was to guess, I'd say that Sweetheart had her throat cut from ear to ear."

"Oh, Christ!"

"You got a tongue on you. I wonder if he realizes that. He usually likes them quiet and shy."

"Fuck him!"

"Whoa!" Dixie said, leaning back on the fainting couch in surprise. "You got the mouth of a ten-cent dove from Front Street in Dodge City!" She laughed and clapped her hands. "I don't know how that's gonna work out. You'd best clean it up, sweetheart, or you might just end up like Sweetheart. Or... maybe he likes it. Change of pace. Maybe he likes the idea of taming a polecat."

"He'll never tame me. If he comes near me, I'll break a glass or a bottle or something, and carve out his liver!"

Again, Dixie laughed. That infuriated Jennie. She looked at the door flanking Dixie, and asked, "Who has the key to that door?"

"I do. And if you think you're going to get it off me, you'd better think again. You might be tough, Miss Jennie From the Mountains, but I'm tougher. Besides, if you somehow made it out of this room, out of the building, Quentin would have you run down long, long before you could make it a block away. Even if you made it out of town, which you wouldn't, there'd be nowhere for you to hide from Quentin Burnett."

Jennie stared at the door, then, deciding she'd have to

take her time to plan a means of escape, her thoughts returned to the three other girls who'd been in her position. "What happened to Sweetheart's baby?"

"Burnett gave it away. Just like that. He didn't bat an eye. Just told me to get rid of it, so I found a poor couple in town who said they'd take the child."

"What happened to the next wife? Surely she didn't have time to grow old."

"Oh, no—she wasn't as old as you... when she killed herself."

Jennie had turned her gaze to the gable window, but now she jerked her startled eyes back to Dixie.

"That's right," Dixie said, answering the unasked question. "Quentin can be... um... difficult... and you just have to accept that. The next girl, a lovely Mexican from a nice family in New Mexico, was bought and paid for. Burnett had been invited to the family's house in Las Vegas on a business trip, and he offered the girl's father a thousand dollars for her. But apparently she'd loved another. She could never get that boy out of her head. She told me all about him. Countless times. She wanted nothing more than to get back to him. When she realized that that was impossible, she hung herself from Burnett's third-floor balcony."

"I can understand that," Jennie said. "I'll do the same thing if he forces me to marry him... or to share his bed. I'll kill myself."

"That's why I'm here," Dixie said. "To make sure that doesn't happen."

"Trust me," Jennie said, rising from the cold water. "That would be a last resort. I don't intend to let him win. I intend to get out of here. My sister and brother need me. What Burnett's doing is illegal. I don't care if the U.S. marshal is in cahoots with him. Not all the law can be. Kidnapping and murder is illegal, and I'm gonna see he pays the price."

She glanced toward the bed. "Hand me the towel."

"He sure picked a wildcat in you," Dixie said, rising from the fainting couch and reaching for the towel. Her eyes drifted up and down Jennie standing naked and wet in the tub. "What a lovely body you have. He'll enjoy you, rest assured. He enjoyed me for a time."

Jennie thought she detected a vague longing in the older woman's voice.

As she took the towel and held it against her breasts, she said, "You... sound... like... you miss... being his *wife*."

Dixie looked thoughtful for a moment, idly braiding a lock of her long hair with the long tail of the black silk bandanna. "You wouldn't understand anything about me. I didn't come from a family. I didn't come from a good place. I was an orphan. I started working the line when I was all of thirteen. When I was fifteen, Burnett chose me... me, of all the girls working for him... to come upstairs."

A faint smile pulled at her mouth. "To become his wife... his second one. I felt honored. And secure."

"But he was so much older."

"So were most of the men I spread my legs for, darlin' girl," Dixie said, placing a hand on Jennie's cheek. "At least I had money... and comforts... and security. Until he got tired of me and brought in another. He'll get tired of you, too, in time."

She slid the towel away from Jennie's breasts, coolly appraising the lithe, buxom girl before her. "Despite the loveliness of your body."

She brushed a thumb across Jennie's left nipple.

Jennie pulled the towel back against her, repelled by the woman's touch.

"Don't worry, pretty girl," Dixie said, making her voice drag with cynicism. "In time your tits will sag. Your face will wrinkle. Your voice will deepen. And then he'll send you back down to the second story, and you'll be spreading your legs for the old salts who can't afford the younger, more expensive girls."

Jennie thought about that. A chill wracked her. As she began drying herself with the towel, she said, "Why did he pick me, anyway? Of all the girls in this place."

Dixie glanced enviously at the long, supple leg Jennie had lifted to dry with the towel, and then turned away and picked up a hand-rolled cigarette off a small, round table by the fainting couch. She struck a match on the wood-paneled wall, touched the flame to the quirley, and blew smoke into the room, toward Jennie.

"He no longer marries the working girls. After he sent me back down to the second floor, he directed his wife-search beyond the confines of the brothel. I remember the day he saw you. He and I were standing in his office, looking out onto the street. You and your father and brother and sister rode into town in your wagon and stopped at the mercantile for supplies. 'There, that's the one,' he said. 'That daughter of Angus Broyles. Look at her. Oh, she's a beauty. And I'll bet she's a virgin. She's the one for me!' "

"That old goat!" Jennie said, tossing the towel onto the bed and grabbing the powder-blue silk drawers from the pile of clothes that Dixie had laid out for her. "He's as old as my father."

Dixie laughed as she sagged back down on the couch. "That's the whole point, dear child."

"Why doesn't he find a woman his own age, maybe someone who loves him back, if that's even possible?"

"It's not possible. You'll find that out soon enough. There's really very little to love about Quentin Burnett."

As Jennie pulled a thin chemise down over her breasts, she glanced again at Dixie, who wore a wistful look. She held her smoldering cigarette in one hand and was braiding her hair again with the other hand.

Jennie scowled in disbelief. "Don't tell me *you* love him!"

Dixie looked at Jennie, and drew on the cigarette.

As she exhaled smoke she said, "It's more complicated than that. Look, why don't you finish dressing and I'll take you to his room? You might as well get that first night over with. No point in dreading it. He's really quite gentle, and he'll make you feel utterly adored. It won't be so bad... even if it's your first time." She arched a brow. "It will be your first time, won't it?"

"It would be my first time," Jennie said. "But since it's not going to happen... "

"All right, all right." Dixie sighed and dropped a hand to her thigh.

"He killed my father," Jennie said. "He burned my cabin. He turned my brother and my sister out into the mountains." She picked up the low-necked dress Dixie had laid on the bed for her, and held it up in front of her. "And now he wants me to dress like a whore and allow him to savage me. He thinks I'll become his submissive wife. Hah! If I get close to the bastard, I'm gonna murder him."

She tossed the dress onto the bed and turned back to Dixie. "If he tries to kiss me, I'll rip his tongue out of his mouth with my teeth!"

Dixie laughed and clapped again, flopping back onto the fainting couch.

While Jennie stood glaring at her, her frustration

beginning to turn to fear and sorrow, Dixie rose and strode over to her. She stared at Jennie for a time as though probing her deepest thoughts.

She shook her head fatefully. "Don't you see? He doesn't mind your refusal. It excites him. It challenges him. He intends to break you like a horse. Slowly. Savoring every minute. It's when you finally succumb—which you will do—that he'll start to lose interest."

Nodding, Dixie walked back to the fainting couch.

"In time, he'll break you. He'll ride the hell out of you... until he's had enough of you."

"Yeah, I know," Jennie said. "Then I'll end up on the second floor."

Clad in only the chemise and drawers, Jennie sat on the edge of the bed. She fought to keep her fear and sorrow down deep inside her. It was a fight she couldn't win. Her father was dead, her home burned, and her brother and sister were likely wandering alone in the mountains, easy prey for bears or mountain lions.

And Jennie had been locked up by a madman in New Canaan.

She lay down on the bed as the dam inside her broke.

She cried uncontrollably.

CHAPTER 7

HAWK STRODE ALONG THE LAST CURVE IN THE TRAIL dropping into the valley he called home, and stopped.

A puzzled frown carved deep lines across his forehead.

What he saw was not his neat frame house with its white picket fence sitting there at the bottom of the valley, on the other side of Van Hootin Creek. It was a common settler's shack—a brush-roofed log cabin limned in the light of a quarter-moon kiting high above the valley.

Van Hootin's cabin. The one the old man, whom Hawk had befriended when he'd come to this remote valley several months ago to recover from wounds and to take stock of his life, had built nearly twenty years ago.

But of course it was Van Hootin's cabin sitting there. Why had he found himself expecting to find his house in Nebraska sitting here in the moonlight of this high-mountain valley in southern Idaho?

Why was he expecting to find his wife and son here?

Hawk shook his head, blinked, and brushed at his eyes as though to clear his vision. At the same time, a wetness came to his eyes, and a cold fist squeezed his heart. Sadness welled up in his throat. He choked back a sob.

His wife and his son were dead. His house was back in Nebraska. It likely belonged to someone else now. He'd abandoned it soon after he'd put six bullets each into the judge and the county prosecutor who had turned the killer of Jubal free from jail, and then he'd headed west to run down "Three Fingers" Ned Meade himself and hang him from a dead nut tree in Arizona.

Still, Hawk had believed with all his heart and mind that he'd find Linda and Jubal here, despite his knowing he'd buried them both back in Nebraska. His gut constricted. Another sob bubbled up in his throat. He dropped to a knee, scrubbed his hat from his head, letting it tumble off a shoulder, and raked a gloved hand down his face.

Linda and Jubal were not here. They were moldering in their graves, one beside the other.

Despite the certainty that he'd inexplicably felt—or *known*—he'd find them here alive and waiting for him, they were still just as dead as they'd been when he'd left them under mounded rocks back in Nebraska, several long years ago now. The cabin in the valley before him was Van Hootin's old shack, the one the old hermit prospector had turned over to Hawk in payment for Hawk's nursing him through the last few weeks of his struggle with an illness that had seemed to eat him from the inside out.

Hawk wept for a time, his face in his hands, shoulders jerking.

Then a strange incredulity and fear began to rise beneath his sorrow, squeezing it aside.

Why had he been so certain he would find his wife and son here?

Was he going—or had he gone—mad? Had his single-minded determination to kill evildoers like "Three Fingers" Ned Meade, long after Ned Meade himself was dead, ruptured a wall that had stood between sanity and total looniness inside of him?

Had his zealous determination to continue to avenge the deaths of his wife and his boy and thus assuage his own relentless grief turned his brain to mush? Relieving such soul-swallowing grief as Hawk's wasn't any more possible than Linda and Jubal being brought to life again.

Had his devotion to riding the outlaw trails with his deputy U.S. marshal's badge pinned upside down to his vest—an upside-down lawman riding against upside-down laws and killing upside-down outlaws—turned his brain to mush?

Hawk turned to stare up the ridge, at the pale ribbon of trail in the moonlight.

Luke Morgan was dead, as well. He was no longer on Hawk's trail. Hawk had killed the young marshal himself —the young man whom Hawk had tutored in the art of man-tracking and law-enforcing, to whom he'd been as close as an older brother.

Luke was just as dead as Linda and Jubal.

So, who had Hawk sensed shadowing him back there?

Phantoms. Only phantoms...

He straightened, composed himself, pulled a handkerchief from his back pocket, and blew his nose. He returned the kerchief to his pocket, returned the Henry to his shoulder, and continued on down the trail.

At the bottom of the valley, he strode across the bridge stretched over the creek. He himself had replaced several of the boards that, because of his illness, old Van

Hootin had let rot. A light burned in the cabin's windows across which the flour sack curtains had been drawn.

Hawk tapped on the door twice, then tripped the steel and leather latch, and shoved the door open. The cabin was the same as he'd left it earlier, after he'd spied the smoke. Only the boy and the girl were there, on the bed built of logs and a skinned pine frame against the wall to Hawk's far left. That had been Van Hootin's bed. The one against the wall to Hawk's right was his own.

The boy sat facing Hawk, tipping his head this way and that, listening.

The girl lay with her head on the boy's lap. She had her eyes open. Now she rose to a sitting position, brushed tears from her cheeks with the backs of her hands, and said haltingly, "We... uh... we didn't see no blond woman."

She looked around as though to further corroborate her statement.

"Or boy," added her brother.

Hawk felt his face warm with chagrin. He moved on inside the cabin and closed the door. "I had that wrong," was all he could find to say. He leaned the Henry in a corner by the door, pegged his hat, and moved to the shelves housing airtight tins of beans and tomatoes and some jars of Van Hootin's canned elk meat.

"I bet you two are hungry," Hawk said.

"I'm not hungry," Jacob Broyles said, staring straight ahead.

Mercy shook her head, then lay back down on her brother's lap.

"You gotta eat." Hawk glanced at the wood box to the right of the small, sheet-iron stove. The box was empty. He'd stepped outside to fill it earlier when he'd seen the smoke. "I'll get a fire going. Get coffee going, anyways. I think we could all do with a cup of mud, eh?"

He tried a smile. It didn't lighten even his own mood. He was still thinking about Linda and Jubal, feeling the horror of their being taken from him all over again.

He walked outside and started to gather wood from the stack along the cabin's north wall. Then he remembered his horse. He walked around to the small stable and corral out back of the cabin, at the base of the valley's western ridge.

The grullo stood facing the corral, its reins dangling. The horse turned its head to regard its rider, and gave an eager snort.

The horse was ready to be unsaddled and fed.

"All right," Hawk said. "All right, there, fella."

He continued toward the horse. There was the sound of rustling brush behind him. He swung around and dropped a hand to the butt of the Russian. He left the pistol in its holster, however. There was nothing out there. He'd only thought he'd heard something moving around in the brush by the cabin.

Phantoms. Only phantoms...

Hawk tended his horse and then brought an armload of wood into the cabin and started a fire.

———

MERCY DIDN'T EAT OR DRINK ANYTHING.

When her brother rose from the bed to sit at the table with Hawk, the girl curled up on the bed, beneath the double blankets, for the mountain night was getting cold, and went to sleep. Jacob ate a few bites of the beans and elk meat Hawk had cooked in a pot on the stove, and drank a few sips of the coffee Hawk had brewed, as well.

The boy didn't say anything as he ate. He just stared straight ahead in that stricken way of his. Hawk thought he must know how the boy felt. Jacob really had it worse than Mercy did. Maybe even worse than their sister Jennie did, because he couldn't see. Without vision out here in the mountains, he'd have to depend on others to survive.

Hawk thought there must be no worse feeling in the world than to be nearly totally dependent on other people. He knew how fallible all people were. How fallible he himself was. In Jacob's blind eyes, he thought he could read his hesitation, even his fear, of sharing Hawk's cabin. After all, Hawk had met the family only once and not for long enough for them to get to know him; nor he, them.

And the boy was probably doubly suspicious of strangers, since he couldn't see them and was especially vulnerable to outside threats. In a way, he was like a blind calf on a mountain full of wolves.

Then, again, wasn't everybody?

Hawk didn't know what to say to the boy, so he said nothing. He was somewhat relieved when Jacob cleared his throat and, staring straight ahead across the table and off toward the cabin's far side, opened his mouth to speak.

"Mr. Hollis?"

"We'd best get something cleared up right away," Hawk interrupted the boy. "My name isn't Hollis. It's Hawk."

That didn't seem to surprise the boy in the least. "You're an outlaw, aren't you?" There was a faint trembling in the young man's voice.

"Some would call me that."

Jacob felt around for his coffee cup, and lifted it to his

lips. He sipped the tepid brew, and said, "What would you call yourself?"

"I'd call myself a lawman. One who does things his own way."

"Are... are you a lawman?"

"Some would say no. I say yes." Hawk reached for the badge that sat on a shelf near the table. He took the boy's right hand in his own and placed the badge in the boy's palm.

Jacob "read" the badge with his fingers and thumbs, and frowned.

"The moon and star," Jacob said, frowning. "A deputy U.S. marshal?"

"That's right."

"I don't understand. Why would some say you're not?"

"Long story," Hawk said, hooking an arm over the back of his chair and taking a sip of his coffee. "A gang of outlaws murdered my boy. Jubal was only a few years younger than you. He was a special boy. Like you. Not blind. He wasn't much for readin' and writin', but he had a special ability, like you with your skins. He could carve horses from an early age so those horses appeared to run with the wind."

Jacob smiled. "A wood-carver, your boy."

"That's right. The best you've ever se——." Hawk cut himself off.

Jacob shook his head. "That's all right. It happens all the time. What happened to Jubal, Mr. Hawk?"

"The gang led by 'Three Fingers' Ned Meade killed him." Hawk cleared emotion from his throat. "Hanged him. Ned wanted to hurt me because I arrested his brother, who himself was hanged, but rightfully so. He was a child-killer. Ran in the family, looks like. After

Jubal was murdered, my wife hung herself out of grief. The same day as Jubal's funeral."

"I'm so sorry."

"I ran Meade down, arrested him, turned him over to the workings of the law. The law let me down. The judge and prosecutor were bought off by Meade. I killed them. Then I went after Meade and the other men in his gang, and I killed them all. I did it my own way, following my own laws."

Hawk tapped the badge Jacob had placed on the table. His fingernail made *ticking* sounds on the badge.

He looked at Jacob. Sober-faced, the boy seemed to be absorbing what he'd been told. Jacob curled one side of his upper lip, and nodded. "Good."

"The reason I told you that, Jacob, is because I wanted you to know what kind of man is going after your sister. She's been taken by evil men. No ordinary lawman would have much chance against such men. I have a much better chance. In fact, I'll go ahead and promise you that if she's still alive when I find her—and you know that part of it can't be guaranteed—I'll avenge you all and I will bring Jennie back to you and your sister. And we'll rebuild what you young'uns and your father built in that valley yonder."

"Yes," Jacob said, nodding his head again, and broadening his smile. "Yes, I see. I see, Mr. Hawk. Thank you."

Hawk rose from his chair. "You take the other bed. I'm gonna go bed down in the stable."

"You don't need to do that, Mr. Hawk."

"Son, I've been sleeping with my horse so long, I tend to miss him when we're not sharin' the same roof. Go ahead and turn down the lamp when you're ready to..." Hawk let his voice trail off, cheeks warming with embarrassment. "Damn!"

"That's all right, Mr. Hawk," Jacob said, smiling as he rose from the table. "You can go ahead and turn down the lamp. I'll manage in the dark. I've been managing in the dark for quite a few years now."

"So have I, son," Hawk muttered as he turned the lamp down, grabbed his rifle, and headed out of the cabin. "So have I..."

CHAPTER 8

THE ROGUE LAWMAN SNAPPED INSTANTLY AWAKE AND automatically reached for a pistol. The Russian and Colt were snugged into the holsters that hung from a chair back, beside his cot in the lean-to side shed off old Van Hootin's knocked-together stable.

Hawk slid the big, top-break Russian from its holster and clicked the hammer back as light spread out from the lamp on a small table, under the room's only, sashed window cloudy with dust and spiderwebs.

Hawk eased the tension in his trigger finger.

He scowled incredulously as a pretty blonde clad in a dress nearly the same shade of yellow as her hair turned to him. Only she wasn't turning from the table in Van Hootin's crude side shed. She was turning away from the scrolled oak dresser that had appointed the main bedroom in Hawk's house back in Crossroads, Nebraska Territory.

"L-Linda?" Hawk croaked, having to clear his throat as he stared in utter shock, lower jaw dangling. "L-L-Linda...?" he said again as he slowly lowered the Russian in his right hand and raked his left hand down his face, brushing sleep from his eyes. "Is... that... *you...?*"

"Gideon," Linda said, moving to him from the dresser. "You've been working way too hard, honey. You're not yourself. Look at you. You're all tensed up!" She pulled the revolver out of his hand and slipped it back into its holster.

She sat on the edge of the bed and leaned over him, smiling her gentle, concerned smile.

Hawk's heart thudded as it lightened. He looked around the room.

It really was his and Linda's old bedroom in Crossroads. Right down to the tortoiseshell comb lying on Linda's dressing table, beside the doily on which her pink Tiffany lamp sat. Her nightgown hung from a peg in the bedroom door. Her soft, wool-lined, elk skin slippers that Hawk had given her for Christmas the year after Jubal was born rested where they'd always rested, near the armoire by the door, on the dyed hemp rug Linda had braided herself one winter, as she'd braided all of the rugs around the Hawk family home.

"Gideon, honey," Linda said, leaning on one arm and placing her other hand against his face. "What on earth is wrong?"

Hawk's heartbeat was increasing. He turned to her, feeling a relieved smile pull at his lips. Relieved? No. Hysterical!

Hawk leaned forward, grabbed both her arms, gazed into her eyes, and then scrutinized her face, her beautiful face with the three tiny moles forming a triangle on her neck, just beneath her jaw. The skin of her neck was the color of nearly ripe peaches.

The first slopes of her breasts shone above the bodice of her yellow, laced-edged dress, the one she usually wore in the summer. There was a faint blemish at the very top of her right breast, nearly as low as the crease between both bosoms.

Hawk ran his hands up and down her arms, over the sleeves of her dress.

"You're alive! Linda, you're really alive, aren't you?" Hawk sandwiched her face in his big, red-brown hands and stared deeply into her eyes again. Indeed, they were her eyes. Linda's eyes. He had every little fleck and swirl in both irises memorized. "You're alive!"

"Yes, Gideon," Linda said, frowning at him a little skeptically but also quirking an amused but cautious smile. "I'm alive. Just like you're alive!"

Hawk placed his head against her bosom, tipping an ear to her chest.

"Gid—"

"Shhh!"

Hawk listened. He could hear the soft thudding of her heart beneath the slow rise and fall of her breasts. Tears came to his eyes. He blinked them away as he lifted his head to gaze into his wife's beautiful face once more.

"Jubal...?" he asked.

"I just put him to bed. Like I told you I would, just before you headed up to bed early. Now, why don't you lie back down...?"

"I have to see." Hawk swept the covers back, dropped his feet to the wooden floor—a floor that seemed so inestimably solid and real beneath his bare feet!—and started toward the door. He took only two steps before, laughing, he swung back around, grabbed Linda around the shoulders, and kissed her hungrily, sucking her lips, tasting her, sliding his tongue into her mouth to feel her tongue against his.

He could smell her and taste her and feel her in his

arms. She smelled and tasted and felt just as she had before.

"You really are alive!"

"Oh, Gid, you must have been having a terrible nightmare!"

"Wait—I'll be right back. I just... I just have to go have a look at..."

He let his voice trail off as he walked out of his and Linda's room, and stopped outside their son's door. Linda had left it cracked three inches, just like Jubal liked it.

The sensitive boy didn't like sleeping behind a closed door. He didn't want a closed door coming between him and the security of his parents right across the hall.

Hawk nudged open the door. The light from his and Linda's room inched into the darkness to touch the brown-haired head of their child lying in his bed and covered with a tied patchwork quilt of red and blue and white. Jubal had pulled the covers up to his nose, just like he always did. He lay on his side, curled beneath the bedcovers.

On the shelf above him lay seven or eight of his horse carvings. All could have been done by a master craftsman. But, then, they had been done by a master craftsman. Jubal didn't do well at school. His teacher called him "slow," in fact. But he could carve a horse so the horse appeared a living, breathing animal a man could saddle or throw a buggy hitch to.

Jubal's covers rose and fell slightly as the boy breathed.

Hawk went over and knelt beside the bed. He lightly placed his hand on Jubal's head, feeling the silky softness of the boy's hair, which was a compromise between his mother's blond hair and his father's half-breed dark-brown hair, for Hawk was the son of a Ute war chief and a white mother.

"Oh, Jube," Hawk whispered, more tears dribbling down his cheeks. He felt a tightness in his throat. "Oh, Jubal, you're alive! Oh, god, boy—I've missed you so much. You'll never know how much your father missed you!"

Hawk wanted to take the boy in his arms and hug him tightly and forever, but he restrained himself. The boy needed his sleep. Days of school and chores afterward were long and hard for Jubal Hawk, who weathered the storm of life well for one so fragile and sensitive.

Inside, though, he had Hawk's Indian toughness and the stalwart resolve of his mother's Texas pioneer stock.

Hawk lowered his head and very gently planted a kiss on Jubal's left temple.

The boy stirred, moving a little beneath the blankets and groaning deep in his throat.

"Sleep tight, my son," Hawk whispered, rising. "I love you more than you'll ever know, boy. Tomorrow, after school and chores, I'm gonna take you fishin'."

He stood staring down at his sleeping boy. He looked around at all the horses displayed here and there about the room, and at the several skins that Hawk had helped the boy tan over the past couple of years.

A dream.

All of his misery had been merely a dream.

A nightmare.

"Three Fingers" Ned Meade had not hung Jubal. Linda had not hung herself out of grief after Jubal's funeral. There had been no funeral.

Jubal was alive.

Linda was alive.

They were *both* alive! Their deaths and Hawk's years of wandering homeless, with only his horse and his guns for companions... all the years of hunting bad men and killing them—all just a dream.

Knife-Hand Monjosa and the Kilroy/Jones Gang and Estella, the devil's whore—and the crooked sheriff, D.W. Flagg—all just figments of a torturous, seemingly endless nightmare of wandering and loneliness with abrupt explosions of deadly, bloody brutality.

My god, what kind of a mind did Gideon Hawk possess, anyway, to have conjured such a nightmare or *series* of nightmares?

Should maybe talk to a doctor about that.

Then he chuckled, his mind returning to the relief he felt. The last several years had been a dream. A dream of epic proportions, epic agony, to be sure. But a dream just the same.

Had that long, variegated dream replete with so many ghastly chapters all occurred in only the past couple of hours?

But, then, most dreams occurred just after going to sleep and just before waking.

Stifling the jubilant laughter that wanted to bellow up from his chest, Hawk tiptoed back out of Jubal's room, adjusted the boy's door, and then pushed back into his and Linda's bedroom. "Boy, I sure am glad I woke. You have no idea what a nightmare I just..."

Hawk let his voice trail off.

Linda stood before him naked. Her dress and undergarments hung from the back of the chair by her dressing table.

"Holy..."

Linda tucked her bottom lip into her mouth, and

moved slowly up to him, chin down, her eyes flashing with erotic flirtation. "You know what I think you need, Marshal Gideon Hawk?"

"What's that?"

He groaned when she placed her hand on his crotch, which had started coming alive the moment he'd first laid eyes on her, when she'd turned up the light on the dressing table. Her hand was like a lightning strike to his loins.

"I think you need to relax. And you know I know the best way to relax you"—she planted a delicate kiss on his right cheek, her lips feeling warm and silky and pleasantly moist—"don't you, Marshal Hawk?"

"Oh, yeah," Hawk said, trying to remember back.

Odd, how it seemed that they'd last made love so long ago. Years ago. But it couldn't have been more than a day or two, depending on if he'd been out on the outlaw trail recently. For the life of him, he couldn't remember. And he was too relieved to see his wife and son alive—the seemingly endless nightmare over—to worry about that now.

As Linda rose up onto her tiptoes to press her lips very gently on his, she began to unbutton his fly. Her fingers moved across him, vaguely teasing, building up the fire in his loins.

She nibbled his lips and tugged at his mustache with her teeth. She opened his pants and slid her hand into his longhandles. At first her hand felt cold against him, but it quickly turned to fire as she wrapped it around his stiffening manhood.

She pulled it out of his pants, and then she kissed him more passionately as she stroked him and pumped him, pulling his shaft up between them and against her bare belly. Hawk lifted his hands and caressed her tender breasts, rolling his thumbs across the swelling nipples.

"Sit down, Marshal Hawk," Linda whispered.

When he was sitting on the edge of the bed, she knelt between his spread legs, pumped him for a time and then gave him one of her smoky, alluring smiles before shaking her hair back to one side and sliding her head forward and closing her mouth down over his shaft.

She ran her mouth down, down the length of his hard member until she convulsed slightly, gagging quietly, when the head of his manhood met the far back of her throat. He could feel her throat expand and contract as she swallowed. She slid her mouth slowly back out to the end of his shaft and started all over again.

While his wife worked her slow magic between his knees, Hawk moved his hands through her hair, combing his fingers through the silky, yellow strands, then brushing his fingers across the back of her neck and over her ears. He ran them down her cheeks, across her forehead, and down her long, smooth neck.

She was alive. She really was alive. He'd vaguely wondered if *this*—what he was experiencing *now*—were the dream.

But, no.

There was no denying the sensations he was feeling. He could not be dreaming such tactile and erotic ministrations. He could not be dreaming the sensations of his wife's mouth on his penis, her head bobbing slowly up and down over his crotch, between his spread legs.

Linda's mouth was warm and moist and wonderfully familiar, her tongue moist and pliant as she slid it around him, toying with him, teasing him, manipulating him, gently sucking as she slid her mouth up and down on him, slowly increasing the rhythm and zeal of her manipulations, until he could stand it no longer.

Groaning and tensing his shoulders, fighting back the tide of passion threatening to reach a crescendo inside him, he grabbed her arms and pushed her back away from him.

She was reluctant to leave him. When she did, she chuckled throatily and brushed a hand across her moist mouth.

"I aim to please, Marshal Hawk."

"Get into bed."

"Whatever you say, Marshal."

Linda got into bed and rolled toward him, her eyes flashing in the lamplight while she watched him undress. It didn't take him long. He pulled the covers back, crawled under them, shoved his wife onto her back, and kissed her lovingly on the mouth for a long time, caressing her cheeks with his thumbs.

He nibbled her ears, kissed her neck, and ran his tongue through the valley between her breasts. He sucked her nipples and her belly button, and then pressed his face into the silky muff between her legs. She draped her long, pale legs over his shoulders and ground her heels into his back as he pleasured her with his tongue.

After several minutes, she was writhing and chewing her knuckles, having risen to the bittersweet crest of her passion.

"Oh... oh, god, Marshal Hawk!" she cried, thrashing around, quivering. "Oh, god—oh, Jesus Christ, you're killing me!"

Vaguely, Hawk reflected that while theirs had always been a passionate marriage, they'd never been quite this passionate, and Linda's tongue had never been quite that energetic. However, he chuckled in delight at his wife's lost inhibitions, and mounted her, sandwiching her face between his big hands.

He thrust his hips against hers.

They came together in a long, violent spasm of shared bliss.

Then, breathless, Linda rose to turn out the light, and they slept, entangled in each other's arms. He'd never slept so well in his life.

He woke to milky blue dawn light pushing through the dusty window.

He blinked, jerked his head up from his pillow, and looked around.

He was not in his and Linda's bedroom at home. He was back in Van Hootin's stable. The clothes hanging from the back of the near chair were not Linda's. They were light-blue denims, a lacy chemise, a hickory blouse, and a light-tan Stetson hat.

A pair of fancy, pearl-gripped Colts jutted from the holsters attached to the cartridge belt dangling from a near wall peg.

Hawk's heart thudding dreadfully, he looked down at the naked girl curled against him.

He swept the thick tangle of sun-bleached blond hair away from her plump cheek and her ear from which a large silver hoop dangled. He recoiled in horror when he recognized the face in repose against his chest as belonging to his long-time tormentor, the gorgeous outlaw devil herself, Saradee Jones.

"No," Hawk said aloud. "*No!*"

His heart had turned to a cold stone in his chest.

Saradee groaned, then lifted her head. Blue eyes, heavy with sleep, gazed up at him, blinking. A silver crucifix dangled between the beautiful, full, upturned breasts chafed red from a recent manhandling. She slid her hand across his belly and squeezed his shaft, which, to his own incredulity and against his will, was coming alive again.

"Good morning, Marshal Hawk," she said, teasing him with her words and her hand. "Wanna go again, do you? Good lord—you're gonna kill me!"

CHAPTER 9

IN A DREAM, QUENTIN BURNETT STARED UP IN HORROR as a large, heavy pillow was thrust over his face. He tried to lift his hands to fight away the assault, but his arms had turned to lead. They wouldn't budge from the bed.

The pillow was mashed down hard against his face.

He tried to draw a breath, but it wouldn't come. The pillow was pressing down savagely on his nose and mouth. His lungs constricted. Terror overwhelmed him.

He opened his eyes and sat up sharply, gasping, sweating, his chest aching as his heart hammered his ribs. Beside him, last night's girl groaned, rolled over, and went back to sleep.

Burnett brushed a hand across his face. There was no pillow. He looked around his vast, well-appointed bedroom. No danger lurked in the dawn shadows.

Catching his breath, he smacked his lips. Odd, how real that dream always seemed. He'd swear he could taste the pillow on his lips, even feel some residue of feather stuffing on his tongue.

Suffocation. Always, someone was trying to suffocate him.

But, why? Who?

Why was he constantly, night after night, plagued by such dreams?

Slowly, the fear released its grip on him. He turned to the table beside the bed. He wanted a drink of water. There was no water there, only the bourbon he'd been drinking before he'd made love to the girl.

To last night's girl. Whoever she was. He couldn't remember, though he was sure he'd had Dixie examine her to make sure there were no signs of disease, the bane of whores everywhere as well as their jakes and pimps.

Burnett lifted the tumbler and threw back the bourbon. It burned nicely going down. He didn't normally drink before noon, but maybe he should start. The strong liquor soothed the night terror.

He didn't care for that emotion. He'd gotten too big and powerful to feel it. He'd grown up on the streets of New York where boys were terrorized every waking and even every sleeping moment. He'd left the Bowery and Hell's Kitchen with his pockets and a velvet, gold-tasseled pillowcase full of money he'd stolen from a man of power.

The man, Hans Christiansen, had taken him in off the streets under the guise of offering him sanctuary from the mire and violence of the cobbled streets. But in fact Christiansen had badly abused Burnett in ways the boy never could have imagined if he had not been similarly abused in the ghettos. When he'd broken away from Christiansen with Christiansen's money, he'd vowed that he'd use that moneyed devil's wealth to build a life for himself in which he'd never feel terror again.

He'd live a life in which he was the inflictor of terror, not the receiver. That's how the world worked. You either received terror or you were the inflictor of terror.

He'd come a long way, Burnett had. He enjoyed inflicting his own brand of terror. He enjoyed wielding power.

Still, the damned dream...

Of course, he knew why he dreamt it. One night, after Christiansen had finished inflicting his markedly depraved brand of evil upon young Quentin, and the man had rolled onto his back to go to sleep, Burnett had taken a red satin pillow and laid it over the man's face. While Christiansen suffocated, Burnett had taken an ice pick and plunged it through the pillow over and over again, until there was nothing left of the railroad magnate's face but red mash and feathers.

Christiansen's long, snake-like tongue had dangled out his wide-open mouth, blood dripping off its sloping tip to pool on his chest.

Young Quentin had dressed, then filled sacks with paper money and coins and silver and gold bric-a-brac, including a jewel-encrusted, solid gold pipe the magnate had kept in its own glass display cabinet in his library. Burnett had sneaked out of the house while the man's wife and children—yes, he'd been married with children —had slept, and quickly exchanged his collection of curios for cash that amounted to nearly ten thousand dollars.

With his newfound wealth he'd hightailed it west and, using the money to fuel the comet of his new life, he'd made a name for himself.

Yes, he'd come a long way.

He wasn't as rich as Christiansen, but he owned damned near the entire town of New Canaan and most of the land and even the mountains around it. His ranch up in those mountains was envied by some of the wealthiest men he knew.

Some of those wealthy and influential men were coming to New Canaan to hunt with Burnett, including the U.S. marshal, Blackwell. Blackwell was not rich, of course. No government man got rich as long as he worked for the government. But he did have power. Burnett always invited Blackwell up here to show him off to his rich friends. Blackwell was useful in demonstrating to others how powerful Burnett had become.

"You have to hand it to ole Quentin Burnett. Why, he has a chief U.S. marshal in his back pocket!"

Admiring laughter all around...

Consideration of the hunt brought Burnett back to the moment at hand. He needed to dress and to get his hunting party together, to organize his guides...

The girl in his bed.

Burnett turned to her. He enjoyed a morning ablution of sorts. It always took the edge off the dreams of suffocation.

All he could see of the girl was her dark head turned away from him on the red velvet pillow. A brunette. He lifted the sheet. She was naked. Her brown ass jutted toward him, her knees drawn up toward her belly. The soles of her feet, which rested one atop the other, were much paler than the rest of her except for the crack between her plump butt cheeks.

Mandy or Candy was her name, though he doubted it was her real name. A *mestiza* from Mexico. She'd been shipped up by a regular Mexican supplier from Tucson. A nice lay, though that's about all she'd done—just laid there! She wouldn't last long. If the girls didn't know how to attract repeat business, Burnett cut them loose, sometimes merely giving them a small canvas sack of the clothes they'd come with, and a sandwich, and shoving them out the Inn's back door.

Most often, they simply disappeared. Burnett didn't worry about what became of them.

Of course, he left the trivial work of dealing with the help to Dixie.

What would he do without Dixie? She literally ran things around here, though she did her share of bedroom business, as well. There were some men who didn't mind diddling an older woman as long as she came cheap. Besides, Dixie had her talents that this girl—this Mandy or Candy or whatever in hell her name was—could only dream about.

Burnett missed that part about her. In fact, Dixie was still a fine looking woman. But he'd tired of her. That's why, despite their being married, he'd turned her out of his living quarters and onto the second floor.

At least, he hadn't kicked her out of the Inn entirely. She still earned a rather decent living for herself, Dixie did. Burnett paid her extra for performing all the tedious tasks that were part and parcel of running such a complicated business, and doing all the hiring and firing of the secondary help—the bartenders and bouncers and the men who swamped out the place and ran the gambling layouts.

Even the stable boys.

Dixie was seeing to Burnett's soon-to-be wife now.

Burnett felt a quickening of his blood as, giving himself a quick sponge bath and dressing for the hunting trail, he considered the Broyles girl. Nothing kept a man young like the prospect of fresh blood in his bed. He'd admired the girl since he'd first seen her ride to town with her father to buy supplies from the mercantile.

Jennie Broyles had turned more than Burnett's head, the businessman had noticed. When she came to town, nearly every man on the street got a crook in his neck, and Burnett had noticed a small crowd of men of all ages gathered around the mercantile while Jennie Broyles and her father had loaded their wagon.

The girl had an earthy charm about her. Tan and outdoorsy, with brown hair that flashed red when the sun hit it a certain way, she carried herself well. Not with a queenly insouciance, but in a way that said she had a spirit as big and bold as any man's.

She'd be a fine trophy, that one. Not unlike the trophy head of a regal elk or grizzly bear. Only this trophy would be clinging to Burnett's arm when he invited his moneyed friends to these mountains to dine and dance and then to head up into the higher reaches to hunt game trophies.

Burnett was adjusting his foulard tie when a knock sounded on his door. He grimaced at the intrusion. His hired help knew that he liked to take his time dressing in the mornings, especially after he'd sat up late drinking and smoking with friends. Cursing under his breath, he dabbed more water through his thin hair, which, he noticed with chagrin, was losing more and more of its brown to a grizzled gray.

Oh, well. He needn't worry so much about his looks. His charm and magnetism were in his raw power and dominating spirit. Women were attracted to him in much the way the females of the animal world were attracted to the males of their own species—a primitive draw toward the stud best equipped mentally and physically to provide best for them and to inoculate them with the seed of stalwart children every bit as indomitable as their sires.

After all, you didn't have to scratch very deep for proof that we were all savages.

Burnett closed the door of his sleeping quarters, crossed his parlor outfitted with several game trophies and an oil painting of the New Canaan Inn mounted above the fieldstone hearth, and opened the main door of his quarters. Dixie stood in the dark hall, looking her own somber self. She didn't appear to have had much sleep. Her cheeks were drawn, her eyes puffy.

"I told you to stay with the new Mrs. Burnett," Burnett grumbled.

"She's dead asleep. I slipped her a sedative in some tea I coaxed her to drink... finally... at four a.m."

"If she hangs herself, I'm holding you personally responsible."

"You do that, Quentin. Let me come in. I need a drink. A splash of the good stuff."

"Oh, Christ!"

Burnett drew the door wider and turned away. For some reason he had a difficult time refusing Dixie. She took too good care of him and his business for him to balk at her surliness and unreasonable demands. Besides, she never ordered him around in front of the other help.

Smart, Dixie was. She knew that would get her a black eye and a fat lip... for starters.

"You know where it is," Burnett said, pulling on a velvet rope hanging down behind the deep leather chair angled before the fireplace.

A bell would ring downstairs, and the help in the kitchen would scramble to bring his coffee.

"Well, since you're here," Burnett said, turning to Dixie and throwing his arms out, displaying his fawn-colored, buckskin hunting suit. "How do I look? Anything out of place?"

Dixie glanced over her shoulder at him while she removed the stopper from a glass decanter. She looked him critically up and down. "You're gaining weight,

Quentin," she said, drolly, then splashed whiskey into a cut glass blue goblet.

She strode to him, her lacy wrap and sheer nightgown spreading like wings to each side of her still-lithe frame. She set the goblet on a lamp table, then straightened his tie and, her right eye glinting with mockery, said, "If you keep eating that venison stew I keep having the cook make for you—with fresh cream, as you always demand—you're going to need this vest taken out."

She gave his bulging gut a poke, and winked.

Burnett chuckled, his ears warming. He still couldn't help feeling the occasional pang of lust for his former wife. He was vaguely, unconsciously aware of a very strong pull toward Dixie, though he wouldn't have admitted it to anyone, least of all himself, despite the fact that she was the only woman—only person of either sex, actually—whom he'd ever been able to converse openly with.

There was a click. Burnett turned to see last night's *mestiza* poke her head out of his bedroom. The girl's eyes widened when they met Burnett's and then shifted to Dixie.

As she pulled her head back into the room with a start, and began to close the door, Dixie barked, "Mecina, downstairs! Now! Get yourself cleaned up and ready for business. It's payday out at the Circle 6, and you know how those boys always demand the Mexican girls! They'll be riding into town in a few hours to stomp with their tails up."

"*Sí, sí, Senora!*" the girl cried, hurrying out of the room, chocolate brown eyes as wide as silver dollars.

As she crossed the room, she said something in Spanish to Dixie. Burnett had never learned Spanish but Dixie had picked it up over the years from the Mexican doxies, and used it to communicate with those who had no English. Dixie barked commandingly back in what sounded to Burnett's unschooled ears as fluent Spanish.

The girl cowered, lowering her head, and made for the door.

As she did, Burnett found himself admiring her slender, brown body with small pert breasts, large nipples, and gently rounded hips. Her hair, coarse as straw, hung straight down to just above her splendid ass. She'd not been much of a lover. What a waste of such fine features! Last night, when he'd been bucking against the girl from behind, Burnett had made a mental note to have Dixie give the girl a few pointers.

As the young *puta* slipped out the door and into the hallway, Burnett glanced at Dixie to find her regarding him peculiarly.

What was that look? he vaguely wondered. Reprimand? Jealousy?

He was about to ask when harried heels clomped in the hall, growing louder.

"There's my coffee," Burnett said.

He pinched his pants up higher on his stout legs and sagged into his leather chair as Dixie went to the door. One of the kitchen girls—a stocky, round-faced, German blonde whose name Burnett could never remember—stood in the hall with her little, pale fist raised, about to knock. She swallowed in fear of Dixie—all the help feared Dixie even more than Burnett—and offered the steaming china coffee cup and saucer with a little curtsy and evasion of her eyes.

"Thanks, Madeleine," Dixie drawled, taking the saucer in one hand. It rattled a little, as Dixie had acquired a slight palsy, most likely due to overdrinking and overworking. "Now, get back down to the kitchen.

Tell the cook he'd better have the bacon frying. Mister Burnett's guests will be rising soon and needing to eat an early breakfast before they head into the mountains."

Madeleine nodded nervously, wheeled, the hem of her pleated white kitchen dress billowing out around her barrel-like hips, and hurried away.

"That reminds me," Burnett said as he accepted the coffee cup and saucer from Dixie, "I'd best get down to the dining room soon myself. I have to make sure the guides are awake. They were up far too late, drinking with the rest of us."

"I'll make sure they're up in a minute," Dixie said, sipping her bourbon and dropping lithely into the chair across a cherry coffee table from Burnett. As was her habit, she was barefoot, and as she dropped into the overstuffed leather chair, she drew up one of her nearly bare legs and tucked it beneath her, crossing the other one over the knee.

She closed the wrap around her the way a moth closes its wings.

"I wanted to talk to you about your new wife, Quentin."

"Oh?"

"Yeah," Dixie said, taking another sip from her glass. "I know you like the simple country girls. But you might want to reconsider this one. Send her back to where she came from. I'll find you another one. One you can actually tame."

Burnett grinned in delight over the rim of his smoking cup. "She's that wild, eh?"

"Wild?" Dixie laughed ironically. "This one's liable to cut your balls off and feed them to you, Quentin."

CHAPTER 10

BURNETT THREW HIS HEAD BACK AND LAUGHED.

Odd, how he'd hated Dixie's salty mouth when he was married to her but no longer minded it so much, now that she was no longer adorning his arm but taking on the brunt of the tedious chores around here. Now she was an amusing business partner.

"I'm serious, Quentin," Dixie said, leveling a frank gaze at him. "She hates you. How could she not? You burned her cabin and killed her father! You might have tried a more subtle proposal. You might have gotten gussied up, ridden up there in your chaise, and taken the girl some flowers."

Burnett had been sipping his coffee. Now he jerked his head up, spewed coffee from between his lips, and threw his head back, roaring. Dixie laughed, then, too, and they laughed together, hysterically, for a long time.

They'd never laughed together this way when they'd been married. Now they kept each other laughing for nearly three straight minutes.

Burnett laughed until he feared his ribs were going to break and tear through his sides.

Finally, he and his ex-wife sagged back in their chairs, panting, exhausted.

"All right, all right," Dixie said, finishing her bourbon and pushing herself up out of her chair. "I've had my say, and, obviously"—she chuckled again—"it's fallen on deaf ears."

"Let me go have a look at the girl," Burnett said.

He thrust his hand toward Dixie, who took it and pulled him to his feet. Burnett looked down at her. He found himself staring down into her low-cut sleeping gown, at the twin orbs pushing out from behind the fine silk cloth.

Lust tugged at him. Odd to find himself still attracted to the woman he'd kicked out of his bedroom nearly seven years ago, now. But there you had it.

She was even older now than when he'd dissolved their marriage because he'd needed a newer, younger conquest...

Dixie followed his gaze, then stepped back, flushing slightly, and drawing her wrap more tightly about her shoulders. She shook her hair back from her cheeks. "Are you sure you want to do that? You might not get out of the room alive, Quentin."

"Oh?" Burnett laughed, gesturing at the door. "We'll see about that!"

Burnett followed Dixie down the hall and up the short flight of stairs to the third story. They stood outside the closed door of the little attic room reserved for the disciplining of wayward whores. Isolation was a handy tool when physical punishment proved counter-productive. The girls had to look their best for the clientele, after all.

"We'll see about that," Burnett repeated as, thrusting

his shoulders back, he turned the doorknob and stepped into the room.

Dixie followed him inside.

The Broyles girl lay on the bed, facing away from him.

"Hello?" Burnett said, raising his voice commandingly. "Turn around here and let me get a look at you."

The girl didn't move. Burnett frowned. Was she asleep?

He was about to speak again, louder, when she rolled lazily toward him. She lay on her back, covered with the bedcovers, regarding him with cold, brown eyes that owned a thin sheen of tears. Her cheeks were swollen from crying.

When she spoke, however, her voice betrayed no emotion whatever.

"You want to do more than look, don't you?" the Broyles girl said. "You didn't burn my cabin, murder my father, and haul me off here to this smelly attic just to look, did you?"

She blinked. She stared frankly up at Burnett as though awaiting an answer to her question.

Burnett hesitated. He started to chuckle nervously but stifled it and glanced at Dixie standing behind him. Dixie arched a brow at him as though to say, "See—what did I tell you?"

Burnett turned back to the Broyles girl and again put a commanding edge in his voice. "You're to be my wife. You might as well get used to the idea. When you do, you'll..."

He let his voice trail off. The Broyles girl threw the bedcovers back, revealing her long, splendid, naked body.

"This is what you want, isn't it?" she said, flaring her nostrils but otherwise continuing to betray little emotion. "You want to fuck me. So... get out of those funny-looking clothes, and climb in here. Show me what kind of husband you'll make. I have certain standards, you know. If I'm going to marry the old, fat tinhorn who killed my father, he'd better at least be a stallion under the sheets!"

She angled her body on the bed so that her bare feet were near Burnett's thighs. She spread her legs, giving him a bold, unrestricted look at her muff and the pink petals of flesh inside it.

She raised her hands to her breasts, pushed them up toward her neck, and then lay the backs of her hands against her pillow, to either side of her head with its comely mess of tangled auburn hair.

"For... for... for Christ's sake!" Burnett said, thoroughly taken aback. He found himself taking one stumbling step backward and glancing at Dixie, who continued to look at him without saying anything. She didn't need to. Her eyes said it all.

"Come on!" demanded the Broyles girl, spreading her legs still wider. "Get out of those silly clothes, old man, and show me how you'll satisfy my wildcat desires. That's what you wanted, wasn't it? A mountain wildcat? Well, now you have one. A virgin one, at that. A hungry virgin! You must take the horns with the hide, Mr. Burnett. If it's a wildcat you wanted, it's a wildcat you have. And I have very strong desires that need satisfaction, Mr. Burnett. Come on. Climb in here and show me what kind of a man you really are!"

She'd pushed up onto her elbows, her cheeks flushed with fury, brown eyes afire. A single tear rolled free of the right one and dribbled down the side of her nose. She brushed it violently away.

"What's the matter, Mr. Burnett?" she raged. *"Aren't you man enough?"*

She fairly screamed that last sentence.

Burnett's heart raced. His cheeks and his ears were hot with humiliation. He felt in his loins a weird tug of animal desire for this naked, wild, alluring creature. At the same time, he sort of felt the same fear he'd encountered when, still half-asleep, he'd watched that pillow thrust toward his face, threatening to suffocate him.

As the girl rose still higher on the bed, Burnett lurched around, grabbed Dixie's arm, and said, "Let's... let's go. Let's get out of here!"

He shoved Dixie out the door, glancing once more at the crazed girl now crawling toward him on the bed, breasts swaying beneath her, her hair hanging wildly down both sides of her face.

Her eyes were like those of an enraged feral creature. Burnett stumbled backward once more and slammed the door. Inside the room, the girl let out a shrill, enraged scream that sounded like the scream of a mountain lion he'd once heard as it had pounced on its prey.

He turned the key in the lock and swung toward Dixie. Even she seemed surprise by the venom in the display she and Burnett had just witnessed.

"I hate to say I told you so, Quentin," she said, breathless, laughing incredulously. "But I told you so!"

"Christalmighty!" Burnett said. "*Christalmighty!*"

———

HAWK PULLED HIS WOODEN-HANDLED COLT FROM THE holster hanging from a peg over his cot.

Still curled naked against him, Saradee Jones stared up at him, smiling with annoying serenity as he clicked the Colt's hammer back and shoved the pistol between her plump, pink lips.

She didn't flinch or pull back or otherwise resist the intrusion of the gun into her mouth. She didn't even blink.

In fact, she closed her lips around the barrel, as though she welcomed it there.

Her cornflower-blue eyes stared up the cocked gun at Hawk, her eyes wide and expectant, almost as though she were awaiting the bullet she did not fear. Or knew would not come.

"You," Hawk said around the hard knot of grief in his throat. "It was you. Last night..."

He glanced around as though he might spy his beloved wife, Linda, hiding in a corner. But of course she wasn't here. She was dead. Jubal was not in his bed across the hall. There was no hall. There was no Jubal. The boy was dead, lying belly up in a pine box six feet underground back in Nebraska, beside his mother.

Hawk was in the narrow lean-to addition of old Van Hootin's stable in the Idaho mountains. It was the female regulator and general no-account outlaw, as deadly as she was beautiful, he'd made love to last night, believing in his grief-ravaged, storm-wracked mind that Linda had come back to him.

"You," Hawk whispered, his eyes wide and glassy with shock.

The barrel of the Colt in her mouth, Saradee nodded slowly, staring up at him, the lamplight reflected in her pretty blue eyes—the crazy, taunting, eminently alluring eyes of an outlaw sorceress.

Hawk said, "I told you the next time I saw you I'd kill you."

Staring up at him, eyes winking in the lamplight, Saradee nodded again. She tried to speak around the barrel of the pistol in her mouth. Her words was badly garbled, but Hawk made out what she said:

"Go ahead."

She blinked slowly.

Her mouth stretched a little around the barrel in her mouth, smiling. She was taunting him as she always did. Taunting him with her beauty that masked a devil's heart. The coal-black heart of a demon birthed in hell's burning soup and freed in this world in the form of a buxom, golden-haired succubus to drive men mad.

Hawk pulled his finger back against the eyelash trigger. It would go only so far, however. It was as though the trigger was jammed. It would not go back as far as it needed to release the mechanism that would drop the hammer upon the firing pin to detonate the powder and blast the bullet out of the chamber and through the barrel and into the head of the vixen gazing brashly back at Hawk, daring him to do it.

Knowing that he wouldn't.

That he couldn't.

Because as much as he hated her and wanted to kill her, he was under her spell.

He looked down at her breasts lightly pressed against his belly. Her nipples felt like rosebuds against his skin. He looked at her left hand splayed against his right side, over his ribs and near the silver cross that hung from her neck. Her other hand was pressed heel-down on the cot to his left. Her hair spilled down around her doll-like face to caress him like silk.

He felt such deep betrayal for what she'd done to him last night, masquerading as his dead wife, that he urged himself to go ahead and shoot her and to scour this buxom siren from his back trail once and for all.

But he couldn't do it.

Hawk pulled the Colt's barrel out of Saradee's mouth. Some of her spittle clung to the site at the end of the barrel. He held the hammer with his thumb while, keeping the revolver aimed at her face, he pulled the trigger, then gentled the hammer down against the firing pin.

"She was so real," Hawk said, looking around the room again, vaguely hoping that this was the dream and that if he looked around hard enough... if he hoped strongly enough, with all his heart... he would awaken and be in his room again in his house in Crossroads, and Linda would be the woman curled beside him.

And Jubal would be in his bed across the hall.

Somehow, he knew that wasn't going to happen. Somehow, the storm inside his mind had abated, and he was back in the real, present moment.

And this was his life now—this shabby room, this moth-eaten cot, this outlaw demon curled naked against him, his loins warming against his will as he remembered the vigor of their coupling.

Saradee looked at his midsection. She smiled devilishly up at him and then placed her hand on his stiffening shaft. She leaned over him, the tendrils of her hair sliding across his chest and belly. She licked her lips as she smiled at him again and then lowered her head and closed her mouth around him.

Hawk lay back in surrender, staring up at the low ceiling beams gauzy with spiderwebs to which the black specks of half-devoured flies hung.

CHAPTER 11

"I'm READY FOR BREAKFAST, LOVER," SARADEE SAID AS SHE DRESSED.

Hawk shoved his shirttails inside his pants and pulled the suspenders of his whipcord trousers up over his shoulders. "You know I don't want you calling me that."

"But we are lovers, Gid," Saradee said, turning to him, bare-breasted. Biting her lower lip, she shook out her thin chemise and then dropped it over her head, covering the upturned bosoms. "Whether you want us to be or not."

She strode over to where he stood by the door, his back to the window. She looked up at him, again her eyes glinting mesmerizingly in the growing morning light. "We were meant to be together, Gideon. We're too much alike, you an' me, not to be together... always."

"How'd you find me here?"

Her smile broadened. "I have my ways."

"I want you to leave."

"Before breakfast?" Saradee exclaimed. "That's not bein' a very good host, Marshal Hawk."

Hawk sat down on the cot to pull his right boot on.

"Shut up and leave me. Why do you keep following me? Tormenting me?"

"Because you want me to. Deep down, you know it's true."

"You're an outlaw."

"So are you."

"I have a cause. I kill bad people. People who deserve to die."

"So do I!" Saradee said, as though she were talking to a simpleton. "You know as much as I do, Marshal Hawk, that there's few folks on the frontier over the age of thirteen or so who don't deserve a bullet."

Hawk pulled on his other boot. "Don't you have a gang around somewhere you could drift back to? Maybe some banks to rob in Mexico?"

"My last gang disbanded as soon as we got back north of the border. Dangerous to hang together. You should know that, you bein' a lawman an' all." Saradee touched the deputy U.S. marshal's badge he'd pinned upside down on his vest last night, and pecked him on the mouth. "Even if you are an *upside-down* lawman."

Hawk leaned forward, elbows on his knees. He scrubbed his hands through his thick, dark-brown hair and then lowered his head and laced his hands across the back of the neck. "What's gotten into me?" he groaned. "Last night was so real!"

Saradee stood buttoning her blouse. "It was real, lover. As real as it's always been. Just you an' me."

"I saw my wife last night. In here." Hawk was talking to the floor, mostly trying to work it out in his own mind. "I saw my son... I saw Jubal... in his room across the hall."

"Oh, that's why you went outside. I was wondering. You came back in smiling like I never saw you smile before. It warmed my heart!"

"Oh, Christalmighty—why can't you shut your consarned mouth, woman!"

Saradee frowned, pouting. She walked over to Hawk and knelt before him. "That's no way to talk to the woman who made love to you last night, Marshal Hawk."

"I thought you were my wife."

"Oh, come on, Gideon," Saradee laughed. "No wife ever made love like that!"

Hawk jerked his head up, anger boiling in him. "Can't you understand—I think I'm losing my mind! Last night... I wasn't here. I was back in Crossroads. You were Linda. She was so real I could taste her and smell her and feel her the way I did before. And when I walked outside, I thought I was walking into..."

Hawk let his voice trail off. What was the point in going over it? Especially with one who was as crazy as Saradee. She was likely even crazier than Hawk was.

Hawk reached back for his Russian .44. He held it in both hands before him, looking at it. He turned the wheel with his thumb. "Maybe it's time I finished it."

"Don't be silly, Gid." Saradee closed her hand over the top-break revolver. "You got more killin' to do. Why, you just got started."

"If I'm goin' crazy..."

"You're not goin' any more crazy than the rest of us."

Hawk gave an ironic snort at that.

"The frontier's full of bad men, Marshal Hawk, Mr. Upside-Down Lawman, sir. And you're the man to turn their lights out!" Saradee pulled the Russian out of his hands and holstered it. "Now, then, maybe we'd best go see to the two young folks inside the cabin."

"Huh?"

Saradee ran her hand through his hair. "The girl and the boy in the cabin, Gid. I bet they're up and hungry.

The girl didn't eat a bite last night, though who could blame her, with her father so recently dead an' all?"

Hawk jerked another incredulous look at her. "How did you...?" He shook his head. There was no point in finishing the question. She wouldn't give him a straight answer.

He never knew when she was trailing him. When she *was* trailing him, she was like a ghost, or the shadow of a ghost. Always staying back just beyond the periphery of his perceptions, waiting until just the right moment to make her presence known.

A sorceress. A succubus. Sometimes, a guardian angel, albeit one with black wings.

She always maneuvered her way back into his life when he was at his weakest, or when he needed her most.

A thought occurred to him. He studied her now as she knelt before him, smiling at him, her hands on his knees.

Was she real? Or was she no more real than Linda had been last night?

No more real than Jubal had been in that imaginary room across the imaginary hall...?

Hawk touched his fingers to her face. She felt so real that she had to be real, but, then, if he'd gone mad, how would he ever know for sure?

Saradee closed her hand over his wrist, drew his fingers to her lips, and kissed them. "I don't know about you, Gid, but I'm so hungry my belly's under the notion my throat's been cut." She rose. "Come on, now. No more brooding and mooning around. Let's go in and stir us up a batch of pancakes. I got the fixin's if you don't!"

She grabbed her twin Colt pistols off the chair back and strapped them around her sensually rounded hips.

Hawk grabbed his own shell belt and holsters, and donned them, then set his hat on his head.

The sun was on the rise now, and the increased light pushing through the shed's single window revealed the shabbiness of his quarters in sharp contrast to his and Linda's bedroom in Crossroads.

He looked back at the shabby room as Saradee went out and strode toward the cabin. Then he followed her, his feet feeling heavy, his shoulders aching from renewed grief.

Linda and Jubal had been so real, he felt as though he'd lost them once again.

Hawk followed Saradee into the cabin. She stopped near the eating table and turned to the blind boy and the girl both sitting on the edge of the bed on the cabin's far side. Jacob tilted his head this way and that, listening, his nostrils working as he sniffed the air like a dog.

"The blond-haired woman!" Mercy said, glancing from Hawk to Saradee and back again.

Saradee arched a brow at Hawk.

"Yeah, right," Hawk said. "The blond-haired woman." He grabbed a handful of feather sticks from the wood box and opened the stove door. "Saradee here's gonna whip you up some pancakes. I'll get a fire started and then I'm gonna take a stroll, have me a dip in the stream."

By the time Hawk had the cookstove stoked, Saradee had the coffee pot ready to boil and was working on the pancake batter, chatting with Mercy and Jacob with the buoyant ease of an old friend.

Hawk grabbed a towel, a cake of lye soap, and his rifle and headed out to the stream. He crossed the creek via the wooden bridge and then walked up stream a ways, weaving around trees and shrubs.

When he came to the deep, dark pool that he'd been using to bathe, he dropped the towel and the soap, and leaned his rifle against a blow-down pine. He kicked off his boots and skinned out of his clothes, piling everything relatively neatly atop a boulder, topped by his black hat.

He picked up the soap and stepped off the bank without hesitation.

The cold mountain water closed around him, pinching his lungs and taking his breath away. It was a good, mind-deadening feeling, and that was what he needed even more than a bath. He needed to have all mind-corrupting thoughts washed away by the tooth-splintering cold water.

Feeling better at the palm of the water's frigid hand, he swam around for a while, the jumble of convoluted thoughts fading from his haunted mind, his senses returning. Now he could smell the creek and the air and the pines, and he could hear the morning birds and see the chickadees and nuthatches and mountain bluebirds flitting amongst the forest boughs.

He saw the sunlight filtering through the trees, causing the dew on the grass and on the leaves of the wild berry shrubs to glow like beads of honey.

Hawk moved into the shallows on the creek's far side and lay in the two feet of water for a time, aware of only the creek murmuring around him.

Finally he stood, soaped his chest and belly, and scrubbed his armpits and then his legs and his feet. He felt as though he were ridding himself of sweat and trail grit in the same way he'd rid himself of the tangled, dark web of thoughts that had turned his mind to a lightning storm.

When soap bubbles glistened over every inch of his

large, dark frame slabbed with ridges of hard muscle, his shoulders as broad and hard as a yoke, he lay down in the creek to let the water wash the soap away, leaving his skin scoured and tingling.

He tossed the soap over to where his clothes were piled, and then he lay back against the creek bank, lolling in a foot or two of water sliding and eddying around him and making sucking sounds as it lapped against the bank. He draped his arms across a tangle of roots angling out of the bank, stretched his legs straight out before him, and crossed his ankles.

He lay back, tipping his face to a dollop of warm sunlight pressing down through the trees. He closed his eyes and let only the sounds of the mountain forest fill his head.

A man's voice came to him, swathed in the sounds of the creek and the birds and the whisper of the breeze nudging the branches.

Hawk opened his eyes and dropped his chin, frowning, staring, listening.

After a time, the man's voice came again. It was followed by a horse's low whicker.

Someone was coming.

CHAPTER 12

VANCE DODGE SAT HIS COPPER DUN AND STARED DOWN at the two still, bloody forms of the Miller boys.

C.P. lay on his back, staring through half-open lids at the sky. He had an almost-dreamy look on his face, as though in his last moments, before that hole had been punched into his forehead, he'd watched a pretty bird swoop down out of the sky to carry his soul to heaven. Del was a mess. He's been shot through his left eye. He'd been shot elsewhere, but the eyeshot had sealed his fate.

Both were bloody messes. Someone had killed them hard, obviously without any trouble and without hesitation.

Dodge snorted at the thought of C.P. being swept off to heaven, and spat a wad of chew onto the grass off the right side of his horse.

There was no way either of the Miller boys were in heaven.

That half-smile on C.P.'s face was downright bizarre. Not only because no pretty bird had carried his soul away to heaven, but because it was in such sharp, grisly contrast to the entrails that had been pulled out of C.P.'s belly by some wild creature of the forest. The liver-colored viscera trailed off for several yards through the weeds.

"Somethin' dug out his liver, most like," offered Frank Sunday as he calmly sat his saddle, building a quirley. "Dug it out and dragged it off to eat it. Not long ago, neither. Probably woulda stayed around here to dine at its leisure, but it heard or smelled us comin'. Lone wolf, most like. Maybe an older one abandoned by the rest of the pack. Whoever killed these two polecats gave him a good meal. One he likely won't see again soon. I wonder if he thanked the man."

Sunday chuckled.

Dodge scowled at the bespectacled gunman from Oklahoma. "Well, thank you for that, Frank. That's right helpful—to know that some creature burrowed into C.P.'s belly and ran off with his liver. You know, that's the most I've heard out of you in one shot since we started ridin' together three years ago."

"He's all excited," said George Reynolds. "He always gets that way when he sees blood!"

"I'm just sayin', that's what it looks like to me," Sunday said, licking his quirley closed.

"Again, thank you," said Dodge, his voice edged with sarcasm.

Reynolds chuckled ironically and turned his own incredulous gaze on Sunday. "Since you have such an inquiring mind, Frank, do you have any thoughts about who might have shot C.P. in the first place, making it possible for your wolf to come in and dig his liver out of his belly? That's who we're after. The killer. Not the wolf."

"Who gives a shit about the Miller brothers?" Sunday said, scratching a match to life on his saddle horn.

Cupping the flame to his cigarette, he said, "Those two lowdown dirty dogs had bullets comin'. I'm just a little sorry it wasn't me who shot 'em."

Chick Holt and Hacksaw Campbell had ridden a broad circle around the two dead men. Now Holt and Campbell sat their horses near each other, Holt facing Dodge while the lean, wiry Hacksaw continued to scour the ground with his busy, colorless eyes, the breeze blowing at his long, brown hair.

"I didn't care for the Millers, neither," Holt said. "But they rode with us. Burnett hired 'em for their gun savvy. They were good with them guns, too. I recommended 'em both to Burnett after I seen their cold-steel work in that fuss along the Apache River. That little fuss remained *just* a fuss because the Millers killed the seven squatters who were threatening to burn out Squire Hedges. The Millers shot 'em when they was meetin' at a roadhouse near the river one night.

"Them squatters were ex-Rebs with mighty big chips on their shoulders. Hated Yankee landowners. The Miller boys alone took 'em all down in that barn that night, and burned the barn afterwards. I won't tell you what they did to them graybacks' women, but you prob'ly know."

"What Chick is sayin'," Dodge said to Frank Sunday, "is that whoever shot the Millers must be better than the Millers. And when he shot them, he attacked us. Us and Burnett. He can't get away with it. To *us, now*, he's a rogue griz with the taste for human blood. *Our* blood. We need to track him down and send him off to where he sent the Millers."

"Who in the hell up here could have shot the Millers?" asked Sunday, smoking and looking around speculatively. "The squatters up here is ranchers. Cowmen. They're not gundogs."

Dodge looked distastefully down at the eviscerated C. P. Miller again. "Well, one is. Unless the bastard who done this was just ridin' through."

Hacksaw Miller stood off a ways from the group, his horse's reins in one hand, both hands on his hips. His gray *sombrero* shaded his face. "Whoever he was, he rode down from the western ridge. We seen him sitting that mouse-brown dun of his right here. Looks to me, judgin' by his tracks, he just sat here as though he was just calmly waitin' for the Millers to ride up on him."

Hacksaw moved a little forward and toed the ground between spidery, dusty green wolf willows. The ground between the willows was gravelly, but with tufts of nutritious needle grass growing up through the thin soil. "They stopped right here. There's their prints. The Millers faced the sumbitch, and he shot 'em out of their saddles."

Hacksaw glanced at the two brothers and then gave Dodge a sharp, fateful look. "He had to have been faster than the Millers. And that's sayin' somethin'."

Dodge glanced around at the men sitting closest to him. Anger burned in him. There was also the slight prickling of fear, though he wouldn't have admitted it even if he'd been conscious of it.

To Hacksaw, he said, "Which way did he ride when he left the Millers?"

"That way."

"Toward the Broyles cabin," said Dodge, angrily.

"He came back this way. The same horse—I can tell by the prints—came back through here but a little wide of the dead men. He was leadin' it by now. Someone was leadin' it, anyway. Must've been him."

Chick Holt said, "I bet them Broyles kids was on the horse. Why else would he be leading it?"

"A neighbor, then," Dodge said. "A neighbor who seen the smoke and came to help the Broyles. He stopped here and watched us ride toward town with the Broyles girl. He killed the Millers, rode on to the Broyles place, and probably rode back to his own place with them kids."

"There's a cabin just over the next ridge to the north," said Hacksaw Campbell, pointing. "An old prospector named Van Hootin built it. Had him a few diggin's in these parts. I ran into him a time or two when I was shootin' meat for the Inn. Last I heard he was dead. Maybe someone's taken over his claim."

Hacksaw Campbell had been in Burnett's employ the longest of any of the other riders. He was a good tracker, but he was known to be a little soft in his thinker box. He was more of a follower than a leader. That's why Dodge ran Burnett's wolf pack.

"Well, it looks like we're gonna go see who's home at Van Hootin's cabin." Dodge leaned forward and slid his Winchester carbine from its saddle scabbard. He racked a cartridge into the action, eased the hammer down, and slid the rifle back home. He loosened his three pistols—a Schofield and two Colt Army 44.s—and booted his coyote dun around the dead men and the blood-splashed willows.

"Hey, Frank," he said as he rode, staring straight ahead at the western ridge, "let's go feed that old wolf of your'n some more liver." He gave a mocking grin over his left shoulder. "What do you say to that?"

"You know what I say to that," Sunday said, smoking leisurely in his saddle as he gigged his horse after Dodge. "Just use your imagination."

Dodge chuckled.

He led his men up the ridge, following the switchback trail. He himself was not a good tracker—he preferred keeping his head up and looking forward, and that's how he always defended his lack of tracking skills—but even he could see the relatively fresh horse and boot prints in the pine needle-peppered trail below.

When he'd crested the ridge, he continued to follow the trail through a little open meadow, with more forest abutting both sides. The trail angled out of the meadow and along the shoulder of a mountain. To his right was a deep, brush-choked gorge. To his left jutted the forest-clad mountain slope.

Hacksaw Campbell rode two riders behind Dodge. He lifted his voice to call, "Down in the canyon straight ahead of you is Van Hootin's cabin."

Dodge jerked a hard look back at Campbell, gritting his teeth, silently berating the man to shut the hell up. Did he want to warn their quarry of their approach?

Campbell flushed and looked sheepish.

When Dodge turned his head forward, his heart hiccupped. A black-clad man stepped out from the trees on the left side of the trail.

"Whoa!" Dodge said in surprise.

But he didn't even get his horse stopped before the black-clad man snapped a Henry repeating rifle to his shoulder and aimed grimly down the barrel at Dodge, whose blood turned instantly to ice as he became chillingly aware of the fact that he was going to die right here, right now.

———

HAWK QUICKLY BUT CALMLY DREW A BEAD ON THE lead rider's forehead, just beneath the brim of the man's gray Stetson, and fired.

The Henry punched Hawk's shoulder as flames

lapped from the barrel and the bullet drew a round circle about an inch above the lead rider's nose. The lead rider's horse continued walking toward Hawk as the rider himself jerked violently in his saddle.

He sort of straightened but then his gloved hands released his reins and, eyes blinking wildly, he leaned back and to one side and then rolled down his horse's left hip.

He hadn't hit the ground before Hawk went to work again with the Henry, levering, aiming, and firing; levering, aiming, and firing. Two more riders went flying backward off their screaming and pitching mounts.

"Holy shit!" shouted a lean rider in a gray *sombrero*.

He whipped up his Bisley revolver from the soft leather holster thonged on his right thigh, but his horse pitched so violently that he dropped the weapon and grabbed his saddle horn to keep from being thrown. Hawk drew a bead on the man's head, but just as the rogue lawman squeezed the trigger, the horse whipped violently to its right, and Hawk's bullet sailed wide.

The other two riders fought to keep their horses under control while triggering pistols at Hawk. The horses were pitching too wildly to get off accurate shots. Hawk calmly racked another round into his Henry and blew one of the last two out of his saddle.

Or *sort of* out of his saddle.

The man fell down the horse's left side and smacked his head against the ground. His hat flew off and his pistol went flying, as well. He got his boot hung up in the left stirrup. When the frightened zebra dun wheeled violently, the rider was whipped through the air toward Hawk. The man's boot jerked loose of the stirrup and the man himself flew past Hawk, screaming.

He hit the ground and rolled.

When he stopped rolling and tried to gain his feet, Hawk blew a .44-round through his chest, hammering him back down. A revolver cracked behind Hawk, and, cocking the Henry once more, he spun back toward the dancing horses. There was one more seated rider, but this man was just now swinging down from his frightened mount, trying to keep his prancing horse between himself and Hawk.

He snapped off two quick shots over his saddle but then the horse buck-kicked violently, wheeled, and ran back in the direction in which another rider was galloping—toward town. The fleeing horse had exposed the man who'd last fired at Hawk. Now the man looked dumbfounded by his lack of cover. He gazed around, crouching, making herky-jerky movements, blinking against the dust rising around him.

He turned toward Hawk, who was just now drawing a bead on him.

The man jerked back and raised his hands, the right one holding a smoking Smith & Wesson. "Wait!" he screamed, hatless and dusty, bearded face slack with shock and fear. "Hold on, now, dammit!"

Hawk squeezed the Henry's trigger.

The bullet tore into the last standing gang member's belly. Stumbling backward, the man jackknifed forward and triggered his Smithy into the ground near his right boot. The bullet ricocheted off a rock near the boot and the man jerked his head up as the ricochet turned his left ear to jelly.

"Ohh-*ahhh*!" the man cried, sitting down hard on his ass. Clutching his belly with his hands, he tipped his head back, blood dribbling down from what was left of his left ear. "Ohhh... *goddamnit*!"

Hawk looked around. Three riders, not including the

gutshot gent missing the bulk of his left ear, were down and not moving. Their horses had run back down the trail. One was standing in the meadow about a hundred yards away, reins drooping as it milled, nervously lowering its head to pull at grass clumps.

Hawk racked another round into the sixteen-shot Henry, then held the rifle barrel down along his right leg. The gutshot rider was a big, bearded, square-jawed man with thick, curly, dark-brown hair. He wore a duster over a wool vest and pale-blue linsey pullover.

The man removed one hand from his belly and raised it to his ear, stretching his lips back from his teeth. He was breathing hard, eyes bright with agony. He looked at Hawk.

"Who the hell are you, man?"

Hawk walked slowly up to him, his face a stony mask beneath the broad brim of his hat. He peered down at the gutshot man.

"Gideon Hawk."

The man's eyes found the deputy U.S. marshal's badge pinned upside down to Hawk's buckskin vest. "Christ, you're a *lawman?*"

"So to speak," Hawk said. "Who're you?"

The man threw his head back, snarling like a leg-trapped mountain lion. "Chick Holt."

"You work for Burnett?"

"I... I reckon... I *did* work for Burnett. You killed me, you son of a bitch!"

"I stand corrected." Hawk glanced around at the dead men and then turned again to the dying Holt. "Where will I find Burnett?"

"Don't you worry, you bastard," Holt said between groans. "He'll find you."

Hawk grinned. "I 'spect."

He raised his Henry to Holt's head. Holt closed his eyes and drew his head back and to one side a little, awaiting the bullet. "Oh, shit!"

Hawk finished him with a .44 caliber slug through his left temple.

Footsteps sounded behind Hawk. Pumping another cartridge into the Henry's breech, he wheeled.

"Easy, Marshal."

Saradee came toward him clad in her hickory blouse and light-blue denims, which fit her like a tailored glove. Her hat's braided horsehair chin thong danced across her chest and over the silver crucifix glinting where it nestled inside her cleavage. "I'd just thought I'd see if you needed a hand."

She stopped near Hawk and looked around. "I guess I could have saved myself a trip."

"How're the younkers?"

"They both ate their fill of pancakes."

"I wasn't sure how you'd be with kids," Hawk said, pulling the loading tube out from beneath the Henry's barrel. "I was a little nervous you might boil 'em up and eat 'em."

"Nah, these mountain kids are too stringy." Saradee kicked one of the dead men. "Who're these fellas?"

"Quentin Burnett's men."

"Is Quentin Burnett gonna miss 'em?"

"Probably." Hawk was pinching .44 cartridges from his shell belt and thumbing them into the loading tube. "That's why I'm gonna take 'em all back to him. He might want a last word."

"You're gonna need a hand."

Hawk shook his head. "You stay here with the younkers. Just don't boil 'em up and eat 'em."

Saradee moved up to stand in front of him, fists on

her hips, gazing frankly and a little worriedly into his eyes. "Last I heard, Quentin Burnett was top dog of the kennel out here. You're not gonna ride into town thinkin' it might be a nice send-off for yourself, are you, Gid? Kill Burnett and go out in a blaze of your own glory?"

"I don't see no glory in dyin'," Hawk said. "And like you said, I got a whole lot more men... and some women... to kill."

Saradee smirked as though she'd just been complimented. "All right, then. I'll stay here with the younkers. I promise I won't boil 'em. You say hey to Burnett for me, will you?"

"I'm sure he'll be right flattered that an outlaw of your caliber says hey."

Hawk started to walk back in the direction of Van Hootin's cabin. Saradee fell into step beside him. "Marshal Hawk?"

"Mm-hmm?"

"You like younkers, do you?"

Hawk shrugged.

"Maybe we should settle down somewhere and make a few of our own."

Hawk stopped and turned to her. He stared at her hard. He didn't say anything. He didn't have to.

Saradee sighed and pulled her mouth corners down with chagrin. "It was just a suggestion. Maybe you don't mind, but I don't like the idea of growin' old alone!"

Hawk gave a grunt and continued walking toward the cabin. After a time, he threw his head back and laughed. "What makes you think you're gonna grow old, Saradee?"

Hawk laughed again.

"Very funny," Saradee said, indignant. "You're a real funny guy, Marshal."

CHAPTER 13

HACKSAW CAMPBELL DREW BACK ON HIS HORSE'S REINS, slowing the mount, and glanced behind him.

He was across the meadow from where the gang had been ambushed, and he'd just entered the trees. He curveted his paint gelding and scoured his back trail, panic a living, breathing, screaming beast inside of him.

The man who had appeared seemingly out of nowhere and commenced killing the gang was not behind Hacksaw. Hacksaw couldn't see the rest of the gang, only a couple of their horses that were now grazing on the meadow's north side, at the edge of the pines. He couldn't see the shooter, either, who was most likely the last man standing.

The other four—Dodge, Holt, Sunday, and Reynolds —were dead. Dead or as good as dead.

Campbell's heart was slowing its frenetic pace but he was still breathing hard, shoulders jerking. His lungs felt like sandpaper. His knees felt like warm mud.

Now that he had time to reflect instead of merely react, embarrassment began to slightly edge away the terror he'd felt and that had compelled him to hightail it as fast as possible from the scene of the shooting.

Christ, he'd never seen a man so calmly and casually dispatch others. The big, mustached man in the black hat had stepped out of the trees, turned toward Campbell's gang, lifted his rifle, and didn't give Dodge any chance at all before he blew him out of his saddle. The man had appeared out of the forest like an apparition.

A black-clad apparition with a Henry rifle.

He'd had green eyes. Campbell had noticed that. They were incredibly bright and vivid, looking out from the shade cast over the top half of his face by his hat brim.

He'd stared calmly but purposefully down the long barrel of the Henry repeater, and dispatched Dodge first and then Sunday. Hacksaw would be dead, too, if his horse hadn't pitched and turned as the green-eyed devil in the black hat fired at him. When the horse had wheeled, screaming, and started galloping back the way in which the gang had come, Campbell had given the horse its head.

What had he been expected to do? Turn around and take a bullet for no good reason?

The green-eyed bastard had still been working away with his Henry until Hacksaw gained the meadow.

A green-eyed demon loosed from the bowels of hell was what he'd been. What he *was*. At least, he sure as hell had seemed so.

Hacksaw drew a deep breath, swallowed, and scrubbed the sleeve of his wool tunic across his horse's head mopping up some of the cold fear-sweat. His heart still drummed against his breastbone. If his horse hadn't spooked and run away, Hacksaw would be lying dead with the others.

Just as dead as the Millers.

Still, guilt began working at him now, casting its slithering tendrils across his back. Maybe he shouldn't have run. Maybe he should have at least tried to stop his horse, turn back, and return the green-eyed demon's fire. Christ, this looked bad. His running looked bad. Maybe he'd be better off lying dead instead of having to negotiate the humiliation of having turned tail and run.

But it was his horse that had run. Hacksaw had just been along for the ride...

That's not how Burnett would see it, however.

Burnett.

What was he going to tell Burnett?

Carefully studying his back trail, staring out across the meadow shimmering in the high-altitude sunshine, Hacksaw swung down from his horse's back and squatted, pulling absently at tufts of fescue. He considered his options.

Maybe he should hoof it back to the scene of the shooting. Maybe he should try to sneak up on that green-eyed demon with the Henry repeater, and drill him. If the man had returned to Van Hootin's cabin, Campbell could follow him and lie in wait in the timber around the cabin or in the brush by the creek, and pink the bastard when he showed himself.

Maybe even shoot him through a window.

Hacksaw had never before considered himself a coward. He'd killed a few men. Not a lot, but a few. He was as good with his long gun as he was with his pistols, by god. He'd ridden shotgun for a few stage lines in Indian country, and he'd even ridden stock detective back in southern Dakota for a time. He'd shot seven men in fair fights. He wouldn't go so far as to say he'd never batted an eye at engaging in a lead-swap, but he'd never before turned tail like he'd just done.

Hell, no. Never. He'd met shooters straight on.

But it wasn't he who'd run just now, Hacksaw reminded himself. It was *his horse*.

Doubt bit him with the fierce pinch of an autumn blackfly.

He was a good enough horseman that he could have stopped the paint if he'd wanted to. He could have turned back and drawn his pistol and engaged that green-eyed fiend and maybe even have killed the son of a bitch.

Then he'd have been Burnett's hero.

Instead, his horse had run and Campbell had let it run because, for the first time in his life—since he was five or six years old, anyway—he'd been driven blindly and at lightning speed by the cold, raw, burning chill of sheer panic.

He could think about going back and shooting the green-eyed devil. But even as he did, the fear lingering in his bones and muscles told him he wouldn't.

As if to cement that notion in his brain, he jerked with a start as something moved on the far side of the meadow. Something dark. Hacksaw drew a sharp breath, his heat hiccupping.

Then the warmth of chagrin rose in his cheeks once more when he saw a stout, black branch tumble from high in a tree to drop into the brush beside the trail.

The branch broke into several pieces and bounced.

The wind had picked up and broken off a dead branch.

That was all.

"Shit," Hacksaw said, running his arm across his forehead again. "I gotta get a hold of myself."

That might take a while, he decided.

He took a few more minutes to consider his options. He could avoid Burnett altogether and just ride on out of these mountains. Hell, he could leave the territory. Head for Colorado or Utah or even Arizona, for that matter.

But no. His pride pinched at the notion of more running.

He'd ride back to New Canaan and tell Burnett exactly what had happened. His horse had bolted and Hacksaw had let it run, because he'd seen nothing good in his dying. After all, that was the truth. That was reasonable. The green-eyed demon had gotten the drop on the gang. He'd gunned them all down like ducks on a millpond. Hacksaw had saved himself, and now he could inform Burnett of the killings and where the gang had been ambushed by the green-eyed devil.

Hacksaw could ride back out here with a couple more men and kill the monster once and for all. This way—by informing Burnett of what had happened and by killing the killer—he'd redeem himself.

Convinced he was not a coward, after all, Hacksaw drew another deep breath. He chuckled confidently, spat into the dust, swung up into the leather, and booted the paint in the direction of New Canaan.

———

QUENTIN BURNETT FELT GOOD. NO, NOT GOOD. HE felt extraordinary.

He felt mildly intoxicated. He hadn't had a drink yet today. In fact, he was sitting in the dining room of the New Canaan Inn enjoying a cup of coffee and taking his time with a plate of bacon. No eggs, no bread. Just coffee and bacon.

That was Burnett's traditional breakfast.

Usually, he'd wolf down the bacon in about three minutes and then sit back and read the morning paper while sipping his coffee while the hired help scurried around him, serving other customers. But this morning, he'd eaten only one strip of the bacon and had nibbled the end off a second one.

He felt too good to be hungry.

He felt good despite the fact he'd wanted to be in the mountains by now, hunting game trophies, but his guests were all still sleeping off hangovers with the doves they'd retired with last night.

Why wouldn't Burnett feel good?

He finally had what he'd been looking for without fully realizing it. He finally had a woman who excited him no end. A wild woman—a beautiful, young, wild woman of the mountains—who he was as much afraid of as he lusted after.

What an intoxicating combination!

He felt like a kid with a new toy. Only this toy could rip his head off. Or, as Dixie had so aptly remarked, this toy could, if given the chance, cut his balls off and feed them to him!

Burnett chuckled as he sipped his coffee, blowing some of the coffee over the rim of his cup and onto his bacon.

"Good lord, what're you laughing about?"

Burnett jerked his head up. Dixie stood by his corner table over which presided the head of a massive bull elk Burnett himself had killed. Dixie had finally dressed and combed her hair so that it almost glistened.

The dress was a purple affair of metallic-like material and velvet trim. It was Dixie's customary attire for the daylight hours, when she was running around the place, managing the help. At night she wore something more revealing, to attract and satisfy the small but loyal stable of her own personal clients who still found her desirable despite her relatively advanced age.

"She excites you, doesn't she? All the more so because she wants to kill you more than all the others combined." Dixie smiled. "Including me."

She sat in the chair across from Burnett and leaned forward, entwining her hands on the table and continuing to smile at him ominously. "Quentin, that girl up there is downright dangerous. If you think she's going to marry you, you're mad."

Burnett chewed a strip of bacon, showing his teeth. "I once had an Indian friend. His name was Iron Tail. A Sioux from up north. He only had one arm. He had for a pet a rare, black cougar with eyes as yellow as that ornament you're wearing around your neck.

"The cougar accompanied Iron Tail everywhere. They came into the Inn together, in fact—the cougar on Iron Tail's moccasin-clad heels. I didn't object. They seemed to be joined at the hip, and the beast was a great curiosity. It was the most loyal creature you could ever imagine. More loyal than the most loyal cow dog. It would snarl at anyone who made a sudden move around Iron Tail, or raised their voice around him.

"One time I worked up enough courage to ask ole Iron Tail what had become of his arm. He told me that before the cougar had come to be his pet, it had attacked him while he slept one night in the camp he'd shared with several other Sioux hunters, chewing his arm off.

"When Iron Tail recovered, he tracked the cougar and, after many failed attempts, he finally trapped it. He did not kill it. He sensed in the cougar a special bond. Because it had eaten his arm, it shared his spirit. They were brothers, in a sense. For nearly a year, Iron Tail kept the cougar on a short log chain. At first, he beat it and otherwise abused it mercilessly. Then he started feeding it, but only a little at a time. Sometimes he would withhold food and water, then give the beast just a little food or just a little water now and then.

"Gradually, the cougar quit hissing and snarling at Iron Tail. It started to regard him with fear and respect. Its world, in fact, seemed to consist of Iron Tail and only Iron Tail. After another six months on the chain, Iron Tail released the cat. You'd think it would have run away, wouldn't you? But it didn't. It came over to Iron Tail, who held a spear over it, in case it attacked. But it didn't attack. It gave a purr and lay down at his feet."

Burnett grinned as he chewed another strip of bacon.

"You see, the cougar recognized the feral bond between them, and chose to stay and serve old Iron Tail, whom it considered its lord and master despite, or maybe *because of*, the abuse he'd heaped upon it."

Burnett swallowed the bacon and sipped his coffee. Dixie stared at him, her lower jaw hanging in shock. When she finally found the words with which to speak, Burnett held his hand up, cutting her off.

He'd just spied something out the window to his right.

"What in god's name?" he said, pushing himself up out of his chair and turning to face the window.

Hacksaw Campbell was riding up to the New Canaan Inn, and all around him were saddled horses bearing the bodies of what appeared to be dead men.

CHAPTER 14

BURNETT PUSHED OUT THROUGH THE INN'S BATWINGS and stood atop the veranda, staring out into the street.

Hacksaw Campbell sat his paint gelding in front of the New Canaan Inn, looking dubiously at the four horses milling around him and over which bloody corpses had been slung. Campbell scratched his three-day growth of beard stubble and then turned to Burnett. He opened his mouth to speak but no words came out.

"What in the hell is this?" Burnett said as Dixie came out of the saloon behind him, pulling a dark wrap around her shoulders against the morning's mountain chill.

She scowled distastefully at the grisly scene before her.

"Uh... well, Mr. Burnett," Hacksaw said, haltingly. "I, uh... I, uh..."

Burnett walked down the porch steps and into the street. Burnett stood beside the horse that he recognized as Vance Dodge's dun, and stared at the back of the head of the man slung belly down across the saddle. Burnett grabbed a fistful of the corpse's hair, trying to avoid the blood, though there was so much of it that the maneuver was impossible, and pulled.

The face, slack with death, appeared.

It was Vance Dodge, all right, eyes not quite closed. There was a quarter-sized hole in the man's forehead, just above his nose. The bullet had exited the back of Dodge's head, blowing out a good bit of brains, it appeared, too.

Burnett released Dodge's head. Dodge's face slapped the stirrup fender. Burnett looked at the other horses over which the rest of Dodge's gang lay belly down. All except Hacksaw Campbell.

Burnett turned his exasperated gaze to the gang's sole survivor, and said, "What in Christ's name happened here, Hacksaw?"

Hacksaw glanced around at the death-bearing horses again, and again gave his beard stubble a pensive scratch. "Well... I was ridin' out of the mountains... and... and I heard the thunder of hooves behind me... and then all of a su-sudden I looked back and... and these four hosses were runnin' to beat the band, like they was tryin' to catch up to me."

Hacksaw paused to study each horse in turn, as though he were trying to puzzle them out. "The bastard who... who ambushed us must've thrown Dodge and the others over their saddles, and... and slapped 'em home, and... and they caught up to me, sure enough."

The sole survivor looked stricken.

Burnett wanted to know what he was the sole survivor *of*, exactly. Or *who*.

He walked over to glare incredulously up at Hacksaw, and, fists on his broad hips, he said, "You're not telling me anything I can't see with my own eyes, Hacksaw.

What I want to know is who killed these men. Who shot 'em, goddamnit!"

Hacksaw poked his hat back off his forehead and looked down at Burnett. "You know how Dodge told you about the man he sent the Millers after?"

"Yes, I know, Hacksaw. It was only yesterday. Are you tellin' me the man who killed the Millers killed all of these men, as well? If so, why are you still breathing? Did you stand with the others?"

That seemed to knock Hacksaw back in the saddle a bit. Both literally and figuratively.

"Well, hell, there were just so many of 'em, boss," he said, wheedling. "And... and they sprung up out of nowhere!"

"How many were there?"

"Oh..." Hacksaw raked his hand down his face, scowling as though it were hard to remember. "Three... maybe four," he said. "I can't remember. They sprung up out of nowhere, ya see, boss."

"Just three or four men took down six of the best gunmen north of the Red River?"

"There... uh... there might've been more than that. They was hidden away in the trees when they opened up on us."

"They didn't give you a chance—that it?"

"That's right, boss. We was ambushed!"

"How did you make it out with..." Burnett tilted his head this way and that, scrutinizing Hacksaw's face and body. "...with nary a scratch on you?"

Hacksaw flinched a little at the question. He looked flushed and nervous. His Adam's apple bobbed as he swallowed. "I... uh... I reckon I just got lucky. My horse threw me an' I took cover."

"And returned their fire, I would assume."

"Oh, of course. I fired till I was out of bullets and then, with all the others dead, I took off after my horse. Without ammo, I was no good, and I knew you'd want to know what happened. So I headed for town. When I was halfway here, these horses came gallopin' up after me."

"I see, I see," Burnett said, nodding slowly, skeptically.

He glanced around to see that several shopkeepers and other townsfolk had gathered on the boardwalks and alley mouths surrounding him and Hacksaw, drawn by the grisly cargoes of the six horses as well as the testy conversation between Hacksaw Campbell and his employer, the richest and most powerful man in this neck of Idaho.

"You ran out of bullets, you say?" Burnett said. "Well, look there." He looked at the well-filled cartridge belt encircling Hacksaw's lean waist. "Why, you have plenty of cartridges in your belt loops, Hacksaw."

Campbell looked down. The flush in his long, horsey face deepened. "I refilled those from the box in my saddlebags... after I ran my horse down," Hacksaw said.

"Let me smell your pistol."

"What's that?"

Burnett held out his hand. "Let me smell your pistol, Hacksaw."

"Why, boss?"

"Turn over the fucking pistol, Hacksaw, or I'll have you tarred and feathered and drawn and quartered!"

Hacksaw jerked and clawed at the lone Bisley jutting from the holster belted to his waist. His second holster was empty. He fumbled the revolver out of its sheath, flipped it around so that he held it butt forward, and, with a sour expression, slowly lowered the weapon to Burnett.

The businessman took the Bisley and sniffed the barrel.

By now, the town marshal, Bob Nye, and Nye's three deputies had walked up to stand a few feet behind Burnett. One of the deputies was holding the bit of the horse carrying Chick Holt's bloody carcass. Burnett handed the Bisley back to Nye.

"Take a sniff of that, Bob. Does it smell like it's been fired to you?"

Nye touched the tip of the Bisley's barrel to his thick, salt-and-pepper mustache, and sniffed. He gave the pistol back to Burnett, saying, "That ain't been fired since it was cleaned about a day or so ago."

Burnett held the pistol down at his side and stared stonily up at Hacksaw Campbell, whose shoulders sagged with chagrin.

"My horse bolted when the bastard opened up on us," Hacksaw said.

"Did you say *the* bastard? Meaning there was only one shooter?"

"Yes, that's right. My horse bolted and ran. It all happened so fast and I was so startled, as we all were"— Hacksaw glanced at the dead men surrounding him— "that when my paint finally stopped, I was a coupla hundred yards away. The shooting had ended."

"One man?"

"That's right," Hacksaw said with a sigh. "But he came out of nowhere. And there was no hesitation in him. He just stepped out of the trees and raised that Henry, and... *shit*!... we didn't have a chance."

"One man," Burnett said. It wasn't a question this time. He looked around, speculatively, then gave his befuddled gaze back to Hacksaw. "What'd he look like?"

"Big, tall bastard. Looked like he might have some

Indian blood. Had a thick, black mustache and green eyes. A black hat, a black vest lined with wool. On his vest he wore a deputy U.S. marshal's badge. Only, he wore it *upside down*. I remember that."

"He wore what upside down?"

"The deputy marshal's badge."

"Shit," said Bob Nye, standing behind Burnett. "That's Gideon Hawk."

"Rogue lawman from Nebraska," added one of his deputies, Burl Loman, who held a Winchester repeater on his right shoulder. "Crazy son of a bitch. There's a four-thousand-dollar federal bounty on his head."

"What the hell is he doing here?" Burnett said, half to Nye, half to himself.

"Holin' up in the mountains, looks like," said Nye. "He sees himself as an avenging angel. When your men burned Broyles out, they put themselves in Hawk's gunsights. If he knows you sent them, Mr. Burnett, then you're likely in his sights, as well."

Burnett nodded as he stared off toward the snow-capped peaks to the west, which were glowing brightly now in the late-morning sun. Burnett turned to Nye. "Best form a posse and ride after him, Bob. We got us a kill-crazy wildcat in the mountains, sounds like. Let's hunt him down and bring him to town. I wanna see this rogue lawman. I heard about him in the newspapers. Been on the loose for a while now."

"A good three years," Nye said. "Ever since some judge and prosecutor freed the man who hanged Hawk's son. He's been gettin' even for that ever since. Like I said, he's one crazy bastard. Rogue lawman—bullshit. He's more like a rogue grizzly on the blood trail."

Nye stood gazing nervously, wide-eyed, into the mountains.

"Well, what're you standing here for, Bob?" Burnett said, testy. "Form a posse and let's get after him. Saddle me a fast horse. Seems as though you want a job done right, you gotta do it yourself. Besides, I'm ready to go huntin'!"

"You got it, Mr. Burnett." Nye glanced at his deputies as he turned and walked away from Burnett. "You heard the man. Fetch every rider you know who's good with a Winchester. Griggs, saddle some hosses, includin' the best for Mr. Burnett!"

As the lawmen headed off, Burnett turned back to Hacksaw Campbell. Hacksaw peered down at the Bisley in Burnett's hand. He didn't say anything. He looked like he might have had a constriction in his throat.

Burnett raised the pistol. He aimed the barrel at Hacksaw. He raked his thumb across the hammer, making clicking sounds as he raised and lowered the hammer against the firing pin.

Hacksaw looked down in dread at the Bisley in his boss's thick hands.

Burnett looked up at Hacksaw. "I suppose you want this back."

Hacksaw didn't say anything. He just stared apprehensively at Burnett.

Burnett suddenly flipped the gun in his hand. Hacksaw jerked with a start. But then he saw that Burnett had only turned the gun so that the worn walnut grips faced him.

Burnett grinned as he handed the gun to Campbell, who accepted it tentatively, as though it were a venomous snake. His muscles relaxed as he dropped the pistol into its holster and secured the keeper thong over the hammer.

"Bury these men," Burnett told him. "Give them each a grave with a marker—you understand?"

"I understand, Mr. Burnett. I'll give 'em a proper send-off."

"See that you do."

Burnett would kill the coward later, after his work was done. Why pay an undertaker?

When Hacksaw had gathered up the reins of the dead men's horses, and led the cavalcade of corpses off toward the cemetery, Burnett turned to Dixie, who stood on the porch, staring skeptically toward the western mountains.

Burnett turned to them again, too, and did not like the chill that rippled the skin across the back of his neck.

CHAPTER 15

HAWK DROPPED TO ONE KNEE ON THE ROOF OF A bakery three buildings north of the New Canaan Inn, and stared to the south along New Canaan's broad main street. He was partly concealed from the street by the front corner of the tall building on his right.

As he looked toward the front of the New Canaan Inn, he smiled. Burnett was just then handing up the pistol of the man who'd turned tail and run when Hawk had opened up on the gang. The rest of the gang lay slumped across the backs of their horses milling nervously around Burnett and the man who'd fled.

The mounts didn't cotton to the smell of the death on their backs.

From both sides of the street, a good twenty or thirty townsfolk stood observing the grisly scene in hushed silence. The four town lawmen who'd been standing near Burnett were now walking off in the opposite direction.

Hawk was too far away to hear everything that had been said down there, but he'd heard clearly enough Burnett ordering the lawmen to form a posse and to head for the mountains, on the trail of Hawk himself.

"Crazy son of a bitch," one of the deputies had said. "There's a four-thousand-dollar federal bounty on his head."

Again, Hawk grinned.

Burnett and the others were rattled as well as distracted.

Hawk rose and poked a half-smoked cigar between his teeth. As he walked to the edge of the roof, he took a couple of puffs off the cheroot, to get it drawing soundly again, then dropped into the saddle of his grullo waiting near the bakery's rear wall.

Taking the reins in his hands and puffing the cheroot, he glanced around.

The only people near him were several Chinese of various ages boiling water on outdoor fireplaces, to the rear of the steam laundry and bathhouse that sat beside Burnett's Inn. Two of the Chinese were wizened old men in coulee hats.

As Hawk rode past them, he tipped his hat to the Chinese gents, who bobbed their heads at him. They had too much work to do—likely boiling the bedding from Burnett's saloon and whorehouse—to pay the big stranger on the grullo more than a passing glance.

Hawk stopped the gelding near the rear of the sprawling Inn. He took several more pensive puffs from the cigar as he studied the layout of the place. Finally, he took one more deep drag off the cheroot, dismounted, dropped the cheroot, and mashed it out with a boot heel.

He patted the grullo's neck, letting the reins hang to the ground. "Stay."

He glanced around once more, then climbed the stairs.

At the second story was an unlocked door. Hawk went in, drew the door closed behind him, and found himself somewhere in the middle of a dim hall with red carpet and a similar design of paper on the walls. The bracket lamps had not been lit.

There were few sounds in the musty hall around Hawk, but he heard a man muttering and groaning from behind a door just down the hall on his right. Hawk moved in that direction, wondering where he was going to find the Broyles girl. He paused outside the door on the hall's left side. The door was open just far enough to show him a gray-haired, mustached man sitting on the edge of a bed, naked save his socks.

He was vomiting into the white enamel slop pale he was hugging on his naked lap. A brown-skinned whore lay naked on the bed behind him.

Hawk was about to move on, but then he saw a wool vest hanging from a chair back. On the vest was the moon-and-star badge of a U.S. marshal.

Hawk gave a caustic snort, brushed a thumb across his own, upside-down moon-and-star, and continued walking along the hall, hoping to find a girl alone—one who might tell him where he'd find Jennie Broyles. But all the other doors were closed. The girls were probably sleeping off the drink and sex of the previous night.

Ahead was a broad stairs up which pale light washed.

Hawk paused at the break in the hall, and looked around the corner, over a scrolled, varnished rail and down the carpeted stairs. Below, lay the Inn's main drinking hall. Hawk could see part of the ornate bar and a few tables. Footsteps sounded, echoing in the heavy silence. A woman moved into Hawk's field of vision. She had long, wavy blond hair and wore a dark-blue dress of a shiny metallic fabric. She held a dark wrap tightly around her shoulders, as though she were deeply chilled.

As she reached the bottom of the staircase, she

removed a hand from the wrap to pull her gown above her ankles, and started up the stairs. When she lifted her head to look up the staircase, Hawk drew his head back into the hall. He could hear the woman coming up the stairs. Her footsteps were slow, thoughtful.

Hawk slid his Russian .44 from the holster angled over his belly.

He pressed his back hard against the wall, head turned toward the top of the stairs. The woman entered his field of vision. She turned toward him and stopped with a startled gasp.

Hawk cocked the Russian, grabbed the woman, jerked her toward him, and threw her against the wall. He closed his left hand over her mouth and pressed the Russian against her temple.

"If you scream, I'll drill a bullet through your brain," Hawk said, keeping his voice low.

The woman looked at him over his large, brown hand, her blue eyes wide. She appeared more startled than terrified. Her eyes seemed to own a cast of recognition.

"You know why I'm here," Hawk said. "Don't you?"

She nodded once.

"Where is she?"

Hawk slid his hand from her mouth, ready to close it over her lips again if she started to scream.

"I'll show you," she said quietly, staring frankly into Hawk's own eyes.

"You won't scream?"

"I'm not a screamer, Mr. Hawk."

Hawk removed his hand and took one step back. Instantly, he liked and trusted her.

Holding the hem of her dress above her ankles, she moved tentatively to the top of the stairs and glanced down. She beckoned to Hawk with a toss of her head, and he followed her up the second flight of carpeted steps, this staircase narrower than the main one. The third story hall was as quiet as the second story had been.

Dixie strode down the hall until she came to a door. She opened the door and started up another flight of steps. These steps were mere unfinished planks. Hawk followed her to the third story and to a plain door with a key sticking out of its lock.

It was early-morning or early-evening dark up here. The only light came from two small windows at each end of the hall. This attic area was only partly finished. It appeared to be used mostly for storage—there were scattered, dilapidated pieces furniture, stacks of steamer trunks, several roles of carpet, and dusty drapes hanging from ceiling beams.

Dixie turned the key in the lock and opened the door.

Hawk pushed her inside, and closed the door behind him.

"Did you finally work up your nerve?" said a girl's voice, pitched with dry mockery.

Hawk turned to the bed on his right. The Broyles girl sat with her back against the headboard, staring straight across the room. She lowered the bedcovers to her knees, exposing her naked body. She turned her defiant gaze to Hawk—and frowned.

As her eyes scrutinized him, recognition flashed in the brown orbs, and she pulled the covers back up to her neck.

"Mr.... Hollis...?"

"It's Hawk, not Hollis. I've come to get you out of here."

Jennie threw the covers back and bounded out of the bed, ripping a sheet from the bed and holding it over the front of her well-curved body. She stopped and looked at Dixie. "What about her?"

Dixie turned to Hawk. "Take me with you."

Hawk frowned. "Why?"

"He's crazy. I didn't realize just how mad until today. I also didn't realize that I've been as much a captive as she's been since she got here." She tossed her head toward Jennie.

Hawk thought it over.

"All right." He turned to Jennie. "Get dressed."

Too anxious to worry about modesty, Jennie dropped the sheet and grabbed a pair of drawers off a chair abutting the far wall. While she dressed with Dixie's help, Hawk cracked the door to stare out into the hall toward the stairs. The Inn seemed eerily quiet. There was no movement on the stairs.

He continued to watch the dingy hall until Dixie said behind him, "All right."

Hawk turned to the women. Jennie was clad in a low-cut, cream-colored dress with lacy straps curled over her delicate shoulders. The frock was a cross between an evening dress and a Mother Hubbard. Hawk gave a silent, sarcastic snort. Obviously, the attire had been Burnett's idea. The dress was a cross between something a whore would wear and something a housewife would wear.

"If I can get to my room," Dixie said, "I could gather us both something more fitted for riding."

"No time." Hawk widened the door and stepped through it. "Come on. Hurry. Stay close."

As quietly as he could, he walked down the narrow stairs. When he gained the second story, he stopped at the bottom of the third-story stairs, and cast his gaze down the hall toward the door to the outside staircase.

The hall was empty, silent. Hawk beckoned to the women breathing anxiously behind him.

When he and the two women were halfway down the hall, a door opened just ahead of Hawk, on his right. A lean, gray-headed man stepped out of the room in which he'd seen the U.S. marshal puking his guts into the thunder mug. Hawk stopped suddenly. Both women behind him gave a quiet gasp.

The man donned his gray hat, and, puffing a pipe, turned to speak through the open door behind him. "I'll be back, honey. You be waitin', now, you hear. I enjoyed them French lessons."

He grinned and drew the door closed. The badge on his wool vest glinted.

He turned toward Hawk and started to take one step forward, but froze. His eyes were nearly the same color as the badge. They also glinted in the dull light sifting through the shadowy hall.

Those eyes flicked toward the badge pinned upside down to Hawk's black leather vest. They flicked back up to Hawk's face. The man's thin-lipped mouth opened beneath his thin, carefully trimmed gray mustache.

"God... damnit," the U.S. marshal said, with quiet dread.

Hawk said, "You gonna go back into that room, quiet-like? Or is this gonna be your last dance?"

The U.S. marshal swallowed nervously, but he kept his unflickering gaze level with Hawk's. "Gideon Henry Hawk," he said. "Rogue-fucking-lawman."

"I have to admit that has a ring to it."

"You won't make it."

"We'll see."

Slowly, the U.S. marshal slid his coat back behind the

walnut grips of the Colt Army jutting across his belly from its cross-draw position over his left hip.

Hawk unsnapped the keeper thong from over the hammer of the Peacemaker holstered on his right thigh.

"Oh, Jesus," said Dixie.

"Stay behind me," Hawk ordered her and Jennie.

Hawk stared at the U.S. marshal. The federal man stared back at him, thin lips quirking a thin smile that faded slowly.

The federal man jerked his hand to the walnut grips and then gave a bellowing cry as Hawk's Colt thundered twice, sounding like shotgun blasts in the tight confines and hurling the federal lawman backward, where he piled up at the base of the hall's right wall.

Behind the door he'd just come from, a girl screamed.

"Go!" Hawk said, stepping aside and gesturing for the women to run on ahead of him. "Take the outside stairs!" Hawk glanced down at the federal man writhing at the base of the wall, staring up at him. Hawk's Colt smoked.

The federal man looked at the Colt, then at Hawk. "No," he begged.

Hawk angled the Colt toward the marshal's head and finished him with a bullet through his brain plate.

Again, the girl in the room screamed.

Replacing the Colt's spent cartridges with fresh from his shell belt, Hawk ran to the open door over the outside stairs. He holstered the Colt and ran through the door and down the stairs. Dixie and Jennie had just gained the yard behind the hotel.

They froze, looking about wildly. The thunder of approaching riders rose around them.

CHAPTER 16

HAWK'S HEART THUDDED AS THE RUMBLE OF THE approaching riders grew louder.

"Take my horse!" Hawk grabbed Jennie around the waist and threw her up onto the grullo's back. "Give him his head and he'll take you to my cabin!" He threw Dixie up behind Jennie, jerked his Henry rifle out of its scabbard, and slapped its rear stock against the grullo's rump.

"What about you?" Dixie shouted, casting an anxious look behind her as the grullo lunged off its rear feet.

"I'll be along!"

Hawk watched the grullo and the two women gallop straight off through a fringe of pines behind the hotel. He whipped around as riders barreled out of the gap between the hotel and the Chinese laundry. Hawk rammed a cartridge into the Henry's action, aimed at the first rider exploding from the gap, and shot the man out of his saddle.

He'd been hoping the man would be Burnett himself, but as he'd fired, he'd spied a badge on the man's shirt. He was one of the town marshal's deputies. Hawk dispatched two more riders in less than two seconds after he'd drilled a bullet through the heart of the first one, emptying two more saddles.

That set the rest of the gang's horses pitching and the men shouting, panicking.

One of the riderless horses wheeled to run, but Hawk grabbed its reins and swung up onto the frightened beast's back.

As he did, more thunder rose behind him. He glanced back to see another contingent of posse riders, apparently attracted by Hawk's shooting inside the hotel, explode out of the gap between the hotel and another building.

"There he is!" a burly, bespectacled man in a bear coat and black opera hat shouted from the back of a cream mare, aiming a pistol at Hawk.

Burnett's bullet sailed wide as Hawk neck-reined his horse, ground heels into the appropriated mount's flanks, and rode straight toward Burnett and about six other men on horseback. Hawk raised the Henry in both hands and fired into the yelling, cursing, scattering crowd.

Burnett's eyes grew wide as Hawk bore down on him. "Ach!" the fat man cried, raising his arms as though to shield his face from a bullet.

One of Hawk's bullets blew his hat off his head. Burnett's horse jerked violently. Its rider lost his hold on the apple and tumbled out of the saddle to hit the ground with a loud thud and another scream.

Hawk killed two of the men trying to control their horses near Burnett and then galloped along the rear of the main street business buildings, dodging around privies and woodpiles.

"After that bastard!" Burnett bellowed. "I want him *dead*!"

Hawk grinned at the confused, horrified shouting behind him.

As a pistol barked and a bullet cut the air to his right, thudding into the corner of a frame building just ahead, Hawk swung his horse to the right and picked up a trail that cut through the pines and angled across an open beaver meadow. His galloping horse splashed through a network of narrow streams, and then Hawk was on the far side of the meadow and following the trail up through pines that stippled the first slopes of the mountains surrounding New Canaan.

When he'd ridden what he judged was probably a thousand feet above the town, he reined his mount, a blue roan, to a stop and looked back along the curving trail he'd taken into this rocky, pine-clad country.

These first slopes of the higher reaches, under a cobalt sky tufted with white puffs of snow-white clouds, would have looked like an alpine heaven if Hawk hadn't spied the pack of angry devils galloping up the slope behind him, closing on him fast.

Horses and riders flashed between the trees.

They were still yelling and cursing, infuriated by Hawk's brash attack on them, killing several of their number, and likely further drawn by the four-thousand-dollar bounty on his head.

"Come and get it, you hoopleheads!" Hawk shouted.

Then he grinned, always game for a chase.

He pointed his horse up trail and rammed his heels into its flanks.

He rode hard, climbing ever higher.

But not far behind, the posse kept coming, triggering shots. The bullets plunked into the ground well behind Hawk, screeching off rocks.

He was crossing a stretch of steep, open ground about

three thousand feet above New Canaan when another rifle belched below and behind him. His horse screamed. Its right leg gave. It hit the ground on its right wither. Hawk threw himself wide so the horse wouldn't roll on him.

Dazed, on his hands and knees, Hawk looked up the slope. The horse was breathing hard, frothy blood boiling out of its nose.

"Bastards!" Hawk gritted out, and finished the horse with his Russian.

He pulled his Henry out of the saddle sheath, racked a round, and looked down the slope at the posse riders galloping toward him, two and three abreast. Burnett was about fifth back in the line of twelve or so men.

Using his dead horse for cover, Hawk cut down on them, triggering five quick rounds and grinning in satisfaction as two posse riders went flying off their horses. The others bellowed curses, swung down from their saddles, and dashed for cover.

Hawk triggered three more shots, then looked around for a better place to shoot from.

Up the slope behind him was a nest of rocks with a craggy rock wall rising over it, offering rear cover. The rock wall was about fifty yards away.

Hawk glanced at the posse men hunkering behind shrubs and trees and low hummocks, chomping at the bit to get at him. Deciding he'd best make his move now, before they all got comfortable and started their barrage, he triggered two more shots toward the cowering posse and then started running up the slope.

He traced a zigzag course around trees and shrubs and small boulders. Behind and below, the posse commenced firing on him.

Slugs spanged off rocks and thudded into tree boles.

One nudged the heel of his right boot and another kissed the nap on his left shirtsleeve.

The rock nest was a little more than ten feet away from him now...

He scissored his arms and legs, running hard.

Another slug burned a furrow across his left side, along the top of his rib cage. Hawk heaved himself up off his heels and dove over the rocks that formed the nest's perimeter. He hit the ground and, cursing against the pain in his side, rolled.

Rolling off his right shoulder, he found himself in the small, gravel-bedded, oval-shaped area inside the rocks surrounding it. The posse's rifles were kicking up a near-deafening cacophony. Bullets sizzled around Hawk's head and screamed off the nest's rear wall.

A quick reconnaissance told him there were good-sized rocks to both sides of the open area, as well, which meant Hawk had some high ground he could hold... as long as his ammo didn't run out.

A cold stone dropped inside him.

All the ammo he had was in his .44s, the Henry, and on his shell belt. He'd left two boxes of ammo, one for his pistols and one for the rifle, in his saddlebags draped over his grullo's butt. Since the sixteen-shot Henry was likely almost empty, he probably had between thirty and fifty rounds.

Rifles thundered. Bullets thumped and spanged off the rocks surrounding Hawk's nest.

Hawk crawled up to a slight, V-shaped gap between two of the largest boulders forming the wall of the nest overlooking the slope, and snaked his rifle barrel through it. He set his sights on a man in a red shirt and black neckerchief just now aiming a Winchester from around the side of a stout fir tree.

The Henry leaped and roared.

The man in the red shirt jerked back, dropping his rifle. He disappeared behind the fir for a second, and then Hawk caught brief glimpses of him rolling down the slope behind the fir.

A bullet crashed into the face of the large rock on Hawk's left, and he pulled his head back behind the boulder on his right as he racked another round into his Henry's action.

He snaked the Henry through the V-shaped gap once more and returned the posse's fire, cursing when he saw no more men go down. They'd obviously seen what had happened to the son of a bitch in the red shirt, and they were revealing nothing but the briefest glimpses of themselves as they fired up the slope.

Hawk returned fire, pulled his rifle out of the V-notch, and cursed again.

Three more wasted shots.

Quickly he reloaded the Henry from his shell belt and turned back to the notch. As he rammed another shell into the breech, he spied movement out of the corner of his left eye. He wheeled in that direction, tightening the tension in his trigger finger.

"Hold your fire, lover!" Saradee leaped over a shoulder of the upthrust of craggy limestone, and squatted on her haunches, keeping her head low as the bullets sliced through the air just above her and Hawk.

"What the hell are you doing here?" Hawk barked. "I told you to stay with the younkers!"

"When have I ever done anything you told me to do... except after dark?" Saradee added with a lusty smile.

Hawk canted his head to one side and narrowed a mock-suspicious eye at the beautiful, busty blonde. "You didn't boil 'em up and eat 'em, did you?"

"Mmmm!" Saradee licked her lips and rubbed her belly. She cast a quick glance over the rocks and down the slope. "What you got goin' here, lover?"

"Just a little misunderstandin'."

"Sounds like a big disagreement to me."

"How many shells you got?"

"What I have on my belt, in my pistols, and the nine in the Winchester." She patted the barrel of the carbine in her gloved hands.

"Christ!"

"That ain't enough?" Saradee lay belly down on the ground and crabbed up to peer through a notch between rocks, to Hawk's left. "How many are doggin' you, anyway?"

"Just shy of a dozen."

"Shit!" Saradee cried, slamming her fist against the ground. "I have a fresh box of cartridges in my saddle-bags. I didn't think I'd need it."

"You thought wrong!"

"Don't get your drawers in a twist, lover," Saradee said. "My horse is just down the other side of this slope. I'll fetch the cartridges and be back in—!"

Saradee gave a squeal as she lifted her head above the sheltering rocks. A bullet fired from below blew her hat off her head to hang by its thong down her back. Saradee dropped back to her knees.

Hawk chuckled without mirth. "Saradee, you're purtier'n a speckled pup. But you're soft in your thinker box. You managed to slip in here without getting your pretty ass shot, because I was keeping those boys distracted. But now that they know you're here, you're not gonna *leave* here with your head on your shoulders. Burnett's men are gonna see to that!"

Hawk laughed again and triggered three shots downslope, evoking one yelp before he pulled back as bullets peppered the rocks to either side of his rifle.

"That's all the thanks I get?" Saradee gritted her teeth as she aimed her Winchester down the slope.

"Thanks for what?" Hawk said, firing the Henry.

"For not letting you die alone, I reckon!" Saradee said, triggering her Winchester until the hammer pinged benignly onto the firing pin.

She pulled the carbine out of the notch and started to slide fresh cartridges from her cartridge belt. As she did, she cast Hawk a bizarre smile. "Kind of romantic, ain't it, lover?"

"What is?"

"Dyin' together."

"Dyin' *together*? There ain't no such thing." Hawk aimed through the notch, trying to find another target, wanting to whittle the posse's number down low enough that the rest might give up on him and hightail it back to New Canaan. "We might die shootin' side by side, but we'll still die alone. We come into this world alone, and that's how we leave it."

He fired, then cursed when his target pulled his head back behind a tree bole just in time to avoid the bullet, which merely chipped bark from the trunk.

"We'll get a pine box if we're lucky," Hawk said, pumping another round into the Henry's chamber. "But probably not. Nah, we'll be snugglin' with the snakes, most like. These boys will leave us right here. Food for the mountain lions."

When Hawk had triggered the Henry once more and pulled it back out of the notch, he was surprised to see Saradee snuggling up close against him. She wrapped an arm around his neck and kissed him on the mouth. He discovered that his situation wasn't so dire that he couldn't appreciate the soft, moist feel of the girl's lips against his.

"Hawk, I love you so much that sometimes I fear my heart is going to burst wide open!" she exclaimed, gazing at him dreamily through her big, blue eyes, around which her blond hair was blowing in the wind. "And you know what?"

"What?"

"I think we're gonna float straight up to heaven hand in hand, and those pearly gates are gonna fling wide for us, and angels are gonna be there to greet us, blowin' their golden trumpets."

Hawk studied her, as usual appalled and enthralled by the girl at the same time. He looked at her cleavage exposed by the open first few buttons of her hickory shirt. While bullets continued to screech through the air and hammer the rocks around them, Hawk lowered his head and planted a wet kiss between her splendid breasts.

"You know what, Saradee?"

"What's that, Marshal Hawk?"

"I'm gonna miss you. Not as much as I miss my wife or my boy, but, may the gods forgive me, I am gonna miss you."

"There you are—see?" Saradee said with delight, kissing him once more as the posse's lead sung around them. "You're under my devil's spell!"

"I reckon." Hawk laughed. He could laugh about it now, because he had so little time to live. Maybe ten more bullets were all he had left in his guns.

Then the torture of this life—all the bitter memories and strange hauntings and his hammering lust for this beautiful devil lying here beside him in this virtual stone coffin—would end.

CHAPTER 17

SARADEE GAVE A YOWL AND LOOKED AT HER ARM.

Hawk looked at it, too. Apparently, a bullet had ricocheted off the stone wall flanking the nest and carved a burn across the outside of her upper right arm. Blood oozed through the tear in her sleeve.

Hawk moved to her, startled by his own concern. "You all right?"

"It's just a graze." Saradee blinked slowly and smiled, pleased by the attention he showed her. "I'm fine."

Staying low, Hawk removed his bandanna and quickly knotted it around her arm. He didn't reflect on the absurdity of his concern for a woman he'd wanted dead for years. Nothing had made sense in Hawk's world for a long time.

When Hawk had finished tending her arm, Saradee gave his hat brim a playful tug, and then they went back to work with their rifles. The posse was closing on them, working its way up the slope and yelling back and forth to each other. They were staying hunkered low behind whatever cover they could find.

When Hawk had run out of bullets for his Henry, he used his pistols.

A half hour after Saradee had taken the bullet burn, Hawk sat back against the rocks, and drew a deep, fateful breath. He hadn't been able to reduce their numbers by nearly as much as he'd wanted. Soon the posse would overtake the nest.

"How many bullets you got left?" Hawk asked Saradee, who was just now triggering one of her pretty Colts down the slope.

She sat back against a rock, legs stretched wide before her, facing Hawk.

"Not enough."

"Save one for yourself."

Saradee curled her upper lip at him. "You save one for me. I'll save one for you."

Hawk gave a caustic snort.

She narrowed a suspicious eye at him. "What's the matter? You've been wanting to trim my wick for years."

"You got that right." Hawk smiled, though he really wasn't sure he wanted to see her dead anymore. And that part frightened him. If they had to die, though, they might as well die together. Hawk himself had no fear of death. In fact, he welcomed it.

Saradee grinned, then swung back to the notch between her two covering rocks. Hawk fired several more rounds through his own notch, wounding one posse man in the leg as he was trying to run up the slope.

Hawk pulled back from the notch once more and checked the loads in his Russian. "I'm down to my last round."

"Yeah," Saradee said, leaning back against her own rock, breathless. She ran her sleeve across her dusty cheek. "Me, too."

She holstered the near-empty Colt and crawled over to Hawk. She wrapped her arms around his neck and kissed him. Hawk holstered the Russian. He wrapped his arms around the blond succubus lying across his lap. He tipped her back in his arms, lowered his head to hers, and returned her tender kiss.

He savored the warmth of her lips, the playful press of her tongue against his. She groaned as she pulled him down tighter against her. Her breasts swelled against his chest. He could feel the warmth of her crotch against his own, igniting his desire.

Saradee jerked in Hawk's arms, grabbing one of her pistols from its holster and firing at something behind Hawk. He whipped his head around to see one of the posse men stumbling backward, dropping his rifle and clamping his hands over the blood geysering from the hole in the center of his chest.

The man looked down at the hole, bug-eyed, and sobbed. Then he dropped out of sight.

"Hey, that was supposed to be my bullet," Hawk said.

"Sorry, lover—it was automatic."

"Hold it, Hawk... and whoever you are!"

Hawk looked up to see Quentin Burnett aiming a rifle at him and Saradee. Two other men stood to each side of Burnett, also aiming rifles.

Hawk looked at Saradee. He looked at the Russian in his hand. The revolver had one last bullet in it. Saradee closed her hand over the Russian and pulled it out of Hawk's hand.

"If we can't die together..." She tossed the revolver away.

Burnett glanced at the two men beside him. One was New Canaan's town marshal, the dark-eyed, belligerent Bob Nye. The other was a beefy, young, curly-headed deputy. "Nye, Deputy Loman—get in there, cuff 'em, and make sure they don't have any more weapons!" He glanced over his shoulder and yelled, "Someone, fetch rope. Plenty of it!"

"What—you're gonna hang us?" Saradee asked, leaping to her feet.

"Holy Christ—look at that," said the beefy Deputy Loman as he stepped over the rocks at the nest's perimeter, letting his gaze sweep the blonde up and down. "Where did you come from, honey?"

Saradee spat in his face.

Loman jerked his head back, grimacing. "Goddamn bitch!" He started to whip up the butt of his rifle to smack her with it, but Hawk, who had also gained his feet, smashed his fist against Loman's right ear, laying him out cold.

"Don't shoot him! Don't shoot him!" Burnett ordered Nye, who'd aimed his rifle at Hawk's head and was starting to draw back the trigger. Nye winced, then loosened his grip on the rifle.

Burnett turned toward the five other surviving posse members, who were climbing the slope behind him, their rifles raised, and repeated, "I want this man taken alive!"

"Why, Mr. Burnett?" asked Nye. "The four-thousand-dollar bounty is good if he's alive *or* dead. I say we kill him and hedge our bets. He's a tricky son of a bitch!"

"That he is, that he is," Burnett said, looking Hawk up and down with keen, almost admiring interest. "But he's a rare and exotic creature. Look at him. Look at the size of him. Note the savagery in his eyes. He's a spectacle. He's been hunted a long time—a particularly dangerous and wily predator. Mad, to be sure. No, no. You don't so quickly kill such a brute as this. Hell, no—you trap him, parade him around town, call in eastern newspaper reporters, call in the territorial governors who put a death warrant on his head, throw one hell of a party!"

"I think he'd rather you hanged him," said Saradee.

"Oh, we'll hang him, young lady. That will be the capstone of the party." Burnett looked at her through his glinting glasses, his eyes narrowing lustily as he raked her curvy form with his gaze. "Who are you? What are you doing here... with him?"

"I'm proud to call myself his woman."

"His women, eh?" Burnett glanced at Hawk, who said nothing.

Hawk's mind was focused only on how to get out of the current bind he was in. He could not be incarcerated. Every fiber of his being chafed at the notion. He should have killed himself. For some reason, he'd found himself reluctant to leave Saradee here alone to fend for herself.

Why such chivalry?

In the past there'd been only one thing he'd wanted to do to her more than he wanted to kill her, but now, suddenly, his priorities were being realigned.

Probably more a sign of the madness that was infecting him, growing inside him.

"Two vital specimens," Burnett said, shifting his shrewd gaze between Hawk and Saradee. "It figures he'd choose you."

"I'll take that as a compliment," Saradee said, cocking one boot forward and thrusting her shoulders back, breasts out.

While Nye held his rifle on the prisoners, the deputy placed handcuffs on Hawk first and then on Saradee, securing their hands behind their backs.

"Christ, you are something." Burnett swallowed as he studied Saradee, flushing.

He glanced behind to shout, "Hurry up with that rope. I want these two tied securely!"

The man bringing the rope broke into a run up the slope. All the others were surrounding Hawk, Saradee, and Burnett, rifles aimed. Burnett held his own rifle low across his waist. He was squeezing it as though he were trying to kill a snake with his bare hands.

"You can get that look out of your eye, old man," Saradee said. "Like I said, I'm his woman. No one else's. When he hangs, I'll hang with him."

"Just his woman, eh?" Burnett glanced at the other men around him. A couple appeared wounded, though not seriously. "How would you like to get a peek at these two together, fellas? That would be something to see, wouldn't it? Two savages toiling as though in the gutters of Bedlam!"

The others chuckled lustily. All except Nye, that was.

"I don't think we oughta fool with Hawk, Mr. Burnett," the marshal said. "He's like a wounded griz. There's a reason it's taken years for anyone to run him down despite that four-thousand-dollar bounty on his head."

"Yes, but it's *we* who had the *cojones* to catch him," Burnett said, staring at Hawk again admiringly from behind his glinting spectacles. "And, since we lost a lot of men in the process, we're owed some fun."

"I say we have some fun with the girl right now," said Loman, his lumpy chest rising and falling heavily as he eyed Saradee. He adjusted his crotch. "I'd like a piece of that right now. How 'bout you boys?"

"Hell, yeah," said two of the others at nearly the same time.

Another man said, "Look at them tits!"

"I told you," Saradee said, flaring her nostrils at the

goatish men surrounding her, lusting after her. "Only Hawk beds me."

"We'll see about that!" Loman lurched toward her.

He got Saradee's right boot in his groin for his efforts. It was a sound, devastating blow. She'd hammered the boot's pointed toe deep into his loins.

Loman jackknifed forward, red-faced and howling, cradling his smashed oysters in his gloved hands.

The others laughed.

Burnett said, "She'll do. She'll do right well. No, we'll save her... for later. I got something special in mind for her and Hawk."

To the man who'd come up with two ropes coiled over his arms, he said, "Tie them both and bring the horses. Tie them good. We're headed back to New Canaan to celebrate our capture." He grinned lewdly at Saradee, his eyes lingering on the upturned points of her breasts. "And to have some good, old-fashioned fun."

Hawk dropped his head and put some slack into his shoulders as the man with the rope approached him, a reluctant cast to his eyes. The man looked as though he were approaching a leg-trapped bear with the intention of throwing a saddle on his back.

"Someone hold him," said the man with the rope. He wore a bowler hat, a shopkeeper's vest, and sleeve garters. His left ear had been creased by a bullet, and there was blood on his broadcloth pants leg. "Hold him good. He's playin' possum, but he's a devil! He's waitin' to bust my nose—I can read his mind!"

Burnett said, "Nye, you and Loman hold Hawk's arms. Gibson, Simms—keep your rifles on the girl. If Hawk so much as twitches a finger, shoot the girl right between her big tits!"

The others chuckled nervously, ogling Saradee.

"Boys," Saradee said snidely. "I'm surrounded by boys."

She turned to Hawk and watched as Nye and Loman drove him belly down to the ground and hogtied him. They weren't taking any chances.

When they were through with Hawk, they did the same to Saradee, taking their time with her, letting their hands get a good feel of her curves. Saradee accepted the assault stone-faced. She'd been through it all before.

Hawk lay on his stomach, staring up at Burnett and the others, who were now waiting for the horses to be led from the bottom of the slope.

Fury was a hot fire building in Hawk. But he had to keep it under control, lest it burn too hotly too soon and consume all its fuel. He had to conserve that fuel for later, for when he saw his chance to kill as many of these men as he could and to affect his and Saradee's escape.

Even if he died in the process.

Saradee...

Why in hell was he referring to her in his own mind as his partner?

Ever since he'd first met her, he'd wanted to kill her, to scour her evil but intoxicating presence from his back trail. Now, however, he wanted to save her even more than he wanted to save himself.

My god, had he fallen in love with her?

And, if so, what did that say about the man he'd become?

When the horses were brought up, one was led aside for Hawk, the other for Saradee. Three men lifted Hawk up over the saddle of one of the horses. They bound his hands and feet under the horse's belly.

They did the same to Saradee.

When most of the other surviving posse members

had mounted their horses, Burnett pinched his pants up at his thighs and squatted down beside Hawk, grinning at him mockingly. "We're gonna take you to town and have fun with you, Hawk." He glanced at Saradee. "A whole lot of fun."

Hawk said blandly, "Go to hell, you limp-dicked old tinhorn."

Saradee laughed.

"No, no." Burnett straightened. "You go to hell, my friend!" He smashed the butt of his Winchester against Hawk's head.

Everything went black and painful and loud. The loudness dwindled gradually, but the pain faded only a little as Hawk drifted into deep unconsciousness.

CHAPTER 18

THE PAIN IN HAWK'S HEAD GREW KEENER AS HE FELT himself floating slowly toward consciousness, toward the loud noise he'd heard before. He groaned against the pain of what felt like rail spikes driven straight down through the top of his head.

The noise grew louder.

He realized it wasn't the same loud noise he'd heard before.

What he'd heard before was the tolling of many cracked bells in his head. What he was hearing now was the din of yelling and loudly conversing men. His other senses began coming alive. The smell of cigarette and cigar smoke touched his nose. He could feel himself being rocked to and fro, as though he lay in a rowboat on troubled waters.

Then he smelled something terrible.

The smell was so invasive—the stench of some horrible rotten thing pickled in hog urine—that it was like one of those rail spikes being hammered up through his nose and into his brain. He was catapulted out of unconsciousness, choking against the disgusting fetor, and opened his eyes to find himself in a large, nicely decorated bedroom filled with well-dressed, middle-aged men.

Smoke hovered over and around Hawk who looked down to see his naked body lying spread-eagle on a bed. A small, hairy hand waved something under his nose. There it was again—the horrible hammering stench setting his brain on fire.

"Get that away from me!" he croaked, and the little, well-dressed man with the hairy hand pulled the smelling salts away from him, recoiling from Hawk as though from a suddenly conscious mountain lion.

"He's awake," the little man—a sawbones, most likely —told Burnett, who stood near Hawk's side of the bed, hands in the air, his fists full of money.

Burnett turned to Hawk, grinned, and then turned back to the crowd of sitting or standing men—fifteen or twenty or so—several waving money in the air with one hand while holding drinks and cigars or quirleys in the other hand.

Several sat with half-dressed whores on their knees or straddling their laps. A couple more whores stood near the door to whatever bedroom Hawk was in, fashioning alluring postures while holding trays filled with drinks.

Hawk was slow to get the layout of what was happening... until he turned to his left and saw that what was rocking the bed, making it feel like a rowboat on troubled waters, was Saradee.

She was also naked.

Not wearing a stitch.

She knelt on the far side of the bed, lunging at three men who were mocking her and laughing, lurching forward to make faces at her or to poke her or grab her breasts, then bounding back when Saradee threw herself toward them, snarling and cursing at the tops of her lungs.

Though they were all in their late middle age and holding drinks, their eyes rheumy from whiskey, they were like young boys teasing a chained lynx.

Deputy Loman was laughing and holding a double-barreled shotgun on Saradee.

Hawk looked around, blinking, certain he must be dreaming.

Having a nightmare.

Burnett barked, "He's awake, everyone. The co-star of this evening's performance. Are all bets in?"

A man with shoulder-length silver hair parted on one side leaned forward on his silver-handled walking stick and shouted, "I got a thousand says he'll finish within two minutes when he gets goin' on her, Quentin!" He was grinning at Hawk, his pale-blue eyes ogling the naked captive almost rapturously.

Hawk rose onto his elbows, scowling at the man. He started to rise when a shotgun was thrust into his field of vision from his right. Town Marshal Bob Nye grinned down the length of his own double-barreled shotgun at Hawk, bald threat in the man's flat gaze.

"Go ahead, Hawk," Nye snarled. "Go ahead—try somethin'. I want ya to!"

"Easy, Marshal—easy!" reprimanded Burnett. "Only shoot him if he steps off the bed. We got us a festive night ahead!" Burnett turned to the man with thick, silver hair. "A thousand for under two minutes it is!"

Burnett took the man's money, then turned to Hawk. Burnett pointed at the silver-haired gent, and said,

"Know who that is, Mr. Hawk? That there is the territorial governor of Idaho. Showed up late today to join my hunting party, and decided to join tonight's private, by-invitation-only festivities!"

Hawk looked at the obviously moneyed crowd around him. He blinked against the wafting smoke. The room was thick and hot and it smelled of sweat and drink and the whores' mingling and conflicting perfumes.

The men in the room must be part of Burnett's hunting party.

They were postponing the hunt to privately gamble on something so repulsive that Hawk couldn't wrap his mind around exactly what it was.

Hawk turned to Saradee, who glanced over her shoulder at him and then sank down onto her butt, putting her back to the headboard. She raised her knees to her breasts, and hugged them, covering herself from the glassy-eyed oglers as much as possible.

She wore nothing. There were no bedcovers. The only bedding at all were two silk-covered pillows and the red silk sheet beneath her and Hawk.

"Welcome to the party, lover," she said with a brittle grin. "I thought you were gonna sleep through the whole thing, damn ya!"

Hawk looked around again, fury a wild animal growing inside of him. He looked at Nye, still aiming the shotgun at him. He wondered if he could grab the gut-shredder before Nye shredded him.

The thought must have shown itself in his eyes.

"Look out—he's gonna make a leap for it!" yelled one of the moneyed crowd, pointing apprehensively at Hawk.

"Not to worry," Burnett assured the man, holding up a placating hand. "If he steps foot off the bed, Nye will blast him to Kingdom Come. Same for the girl. Keep your eyes on her at all times, Deputy Loman. I'm sure that won't be hard!" Burnett added, laughing, evoking more laughter from the crowd.

"Relax, Hawk," Saradee said. "We're not goin' anywhere. I sure would like to get my hands on one of those shotguns, though." She turned her smoldering gaze to Burnett. "You know just where I'd like to stick it and pull both triggers!"

Hawk looked at Burnett. Fury exploded in him in once more, but he reined it back. He didn't want to die here, like this—naked on a bed, a spectacle in a room full of wealthy demons. He had to live so he could kill Burnett.

"What the hell is this about?" Hawk asked, half to himself. "What do they want?"

"Take a guess, lover. Look at you. Look at me. Take a guess."

Hawk stared out at the crowd forming a semicircle around the bed. Most of the rich men were getting their drinks replenished by the scantily clad whores. They were savoring the moment, enjoying the anticipation of the spectacle ahead.

Hawk would be damned if he'd give it to them.

He wasn't some wild animal to be humiliated in some rich man's depraved circus.

"Forget it," Hawk said. "I won't give 'em the satisfaction."

"I don't think we have much choice, lover."

"You heard me—forget it."

"You don't wanna die this way any more than I do, Gid. We gotta get our hands on some guns. We gotta fix that bastard's wagon." Saradee turned toward Hawk. "Pretend they're not here. Pretend we're alone."

She caressed his cheek with the back of her left hand and gave him a sympathetic look. "It'll be okay. I promise. We'll have our revenge, lover."

"Look, look—I think she's enticing him!" someone yelled.

Instantly, the din in the room subsided as the gamblers cast their eager gazes toward the bed.

Hawk looked around the room once more. "Go to hell!" he bellowed so loudly that the lamps around the room rattled. He climbed onto his hands and knees, ignoring Nye, who thrust his shotgun toward Hawk's head, and stared red-faced at the crowd. "You can all go to hell! I won't be humiliated, you sonso'bitches!"

"Oh, I sincerely think you will, Mr. Hawk," yelled Burnett, grinning the self-assured grin again that Hawk wanted so much to scrub from the man's face with one of the shotguns.

The crowd fell nearly silent as Burnett turned toward the bed and pulled a small-caliber, silver-chased, pearl-gripped pocket pistol from the waistband of his trousers. He clicked the hammer back and aimed it at Saradee.

"Do your duty, Marshal Hawk. Perform the act we require of you... or I'm gonna kill her. Slow. One bullet, one limb, at a time." He slid his devilish gaze to Hawk. "You wouldn't want that, now, would you?"

Saradee slid her gaze from the barrel of Burnett's Merwin & Hulbert revolver to Hawk. Her eyes asked the same question Burnett had asked.

Hawk had no idea why, but for the love of him, he didn't want her hurt.

"Take the gun away, you son of a bitch."

Burnett smiled and pulled the gun back. He depressed the hammer and stepped aside.

He turned to the room and said, "Gentlemen, I think

we have two willing participants now. The bets are in!" He gestured to Hawk and Saradee. "Let the game begin!"

The crowd erupted with roars of encouragement and applause.

"Three minutes," someone yelled. "You gotta last three minutes, Hawk!"

"No, no—take your time, big fella. You gotta last *five* minutes—you understand? Five minutes or I'll have to sell my house... and divorce my wife!"

"And leave the country!" added another man.

The crowd roared at the joke.

Hawk turned to Saradee and tried to close out the cacophony in the room around him.

"Christ," he said, placing his right hand on her left cheek, curling his upper lip with fury and humiliation as he stared down at her. "If there was a way, I'd kill every bastard in this room!"

"Don't listen to 'em, lover," Saradee said, snuggling down against the bed and rubbing her breasts against his chest, curling one leg over his. "It's just us. We're the only ones here. It'll be like all the other times."

He could feel the tuft of fur between her thighs prick softly against his belly. He was surprised to feel a wave of erotic pleasure wash from his belly to his toes, even with the crowd staring at him.

Hawk looked at the slender wooden bedposts holding up the canopy over the bed.

"All right," he said. "It's just you and me."

Saradee was massaging him with both her supple hands, smiling up into his face. It was as though she'd shut out the spectators completely. It was as if there really was no one else here but her and Hawk.

Two lovers making love.

"It's all right if you want to pretend I'm Linda," Saradee said in a little girl's voice, brushing the backs of her fingers up across his cheeks to his temples.

Hawk shook his head, grinding his molars. "Be quiet."

"We don't need her here, do we?"

"Goddamnit, I told you to be quiet."

"It'll be all right," she said, reaching down for him again. Her hands were warm and tender, so hypnotically artful in the way they manipulated him, toying with him gently, teasingly. "There, now. How's that? Oh, yeah... you like that. Just like you've always enjoyed it, lover. All the years, and you didn't realize how much you enjoyed it, did you? Making love to a killer?"

"I did know," Hawk grunted. "That was the trouble."

"Because you knew we were cut from the same cloth."

"No."

"Yes."

"If you don't shut up, goddamnit—! If we have to do this, let's just..." He let the thought trail away, shaking his head. "We were not cut from the same cloth."

Hawk was not aware of the crowd's sudden silence punctuated by only a hushed, awful exclamation now and then. Or an appreciative chuckle. He'd almost entirely shut the gamblers out of his mind.

Saradee laughed as her hands continued to tease him to arousal. "I don't think you ever needed Linda. I've always been enough."

"Oh, Jesus," Hawk croaked, glancing around briefly to see the spectators gathering closer for a better view. "Shut the hell up!" he told Saradee, pushing the gamblers from his mind again.

"You don't need Linda anymore. She's dead. I'm here. I'm alive, Hawk!"

"Shut up!" As much as he hated her, or hated loving her, he was continuing to come alive in her hands.

"I'll always be here for you, Gideon." Saradee laughed her sweet, mocking, knowing laugh. "That's all you need to know. That's all you *need*!"

"Oh, Christ," Hawk said as the bittersweet pangs of his rising desire rolled through his loins. "Lord help me."

He looked down between them. He was fully erect. Her hands pumped him slowly but eagerly. The blond succubus beneath him smiled up at him, lips slightly parted to reveal her perfect, even teeth. It was a teasing, gently mocking smile.

A sweetly smiling succubus beneath him, urging his soul on to hell with her. And he was entirely willing to go.

"Lord have mercy on my wretched soul!" Hawk intoned, thinking of his son and wife, though their images were growing harder and harder to conjure. It was as though they were spiraling away from him, disappearing into the mists of forgotten time.

He sobbed as a dam of pent-up emotion burst inside him. He sobbed beneath the cacophony swirling around him.

"Lord have mercy!" he cried.

Saradee laughed. "Good luck with that, lover!"

Saradee slipped him inside her and pressed her hands down hard against his buttocks, sliding him in... in... in!

The room erupted with loud applause, ribald laughter, thunderous encouragement.

Hawk shut it out as best he could as, sandwiching Saradee's face in his hands, sobbing, he began hammering his hips against hers. His rhythm increased as his passion grew.

He glanced at the canopy shaking above him. The posters supporting it shook and swayed.

Nye and Loman stood to each side of the bed, about six feet away, their shotguns sagging slightly in their hands as they watched the mesmerizing spectacle before them.

Hawk thrust his hips against Saradee harder, harder, harder...

The four canopy posts started making soft cracking sounds.

Saradee wrapped her arms around Hawk's neck, entwining her legs over his back.

"Jesus Christ, they're really goin' at it!" one of the spectators shouted, laughing.

"Shhhh!" admonished another of the crowd.

"If they ain't careful, they're gonna break the bed!" another man warned, and snickered.

"Oh, my gosh!" cried one of the whores, aghast. "They're like two... *animals*!"

"You takin' notes, Betsy?" one of the male spectators asked the shocked dove.

A roar of laughter.

Occasionally, Hawk could hear men clapping and yelling instructions and encouragement, as though he and Saradee were boxers in a ring. Mostly, he saw and heard nothing at all. He only felt the heat of his passion rising while an entire universe of grief and anger and self-recrimination hammered away at his soul, pummeling him into submission.

Saradee tried to pull his head down to her, to kiss him, but he resisted. Propped on his outstretched arms, he ground the heels of his hands into the mattress on either side of her beautiful blond head.

She smiled up at him dreamily, eyes glinting in the lamplight.

Then he saw that she was frowning. A strange, incred-

ulous light had entered her eyes. She lowered her hands
to her neck.

Hawk saw that one of his hands was around her
throat.

CHAPTER 19

"Hawk," Saradee rasped, trying to pull his hand away.

Hawk hammered against her faster, harder.

Faster, harder.

Faster...

Harder...

"Hawk," she said, but he could only read her lips. No sound escaped her mouth. His fingers were digging into her throat, pinching off her wind. She clawed at it desperately but she couldn't budge it. Her strength was no match for his.

The crowd roared around Hawk, but his brain registered the cacophony as though it originated from a half a mile away through a dense forest. He could see movement around him as the crowd drew closer to get a better view of the depravity in their midst, but Hawk registered only shifting shadows in the very periphery of his vision.

As he continued to hammer against Saradee, strangling her, she struggled violently against him, clawing at his hands, kicking her long legs at him, desperately trying to unseat him.

But Hawk was immovable. Her desperate struggles only exacerbated his desire.

He kept his hand fast against her neck, digging his fingers deeper and deeper into her throat.

Saradee let her hands flop down onto the bed. She stared up at him. Gradually, the fear left her eyes. It was replaced with a vague amusement even as her face turned from pale to light blue, and her eyes turned to isinglass.

"Christ, what's he doin'?"asked one of the men in the crowd, inching closer and closer to the pitching and swaying bed.

"He's strangling her!" The speaker guffawed nervously. "Good god—you ever see such a thing! Why, he's diddlin' her to death!"

Hawk glanced up at the canopy. It pitched and swayed in time with the bed.

He hammered against Saradee, the heat of his passion rising in his loins. Saradee lay still beneath him, glassily staring, unmoving...

"Lord have mercy on my soul!" Hawk bellowed, tipping his head back and gritting his teeth as the canopy posts splintered.

Hawk held his hips fast against Saradee, his loins spasming. The right front canopy post broke in two. Then the left one broke in two. At the same time, the rear posts were breaking.

The canopy fell down around Hawk's head and shoulders.

"Christalmighty!" Burnett shouted. "*Shoot* the son of a bitch!"

"Don't let him get away!" bellowed another man.

Hawk leaped off of Saradee. He shouldered the side of the canopy off of him. The crowd was right next to the bed. He glimpsed a shotgun held by Loman, who'd lunged forward to shove the gut-shredder beneath the canopy.

Hawk thrust his hands forward, ripped the shotgun out of the deputy's hands, pulled the hammers back, whipped the barrels forward, and tripped a trigger.

Thunder racked the room.

Loman screamed as he was blown off his feet and backward.

Again, Hawk shouldered the canopy up and away from him. Nye lunged toward the bed, aiming a shotgun. Hawk aimed his own shotgun at the marshal's belly and sent him flying violently and bellowing shrilly back against the wall.

Hawk tossed the empty shotgun aside and jerked his head toward the door.

Apparently there had been a pileup that was just now clearing as the men who'd fallen on each other in their frenzy to leave the room gained their feet and ran off down the hall.

Two doves who'd been hammered under the fleeing gamblers' feet were quietly sobbing on the floor. They didn't look so much injured as scared. They both cast bright-eyed, fearful gazes toward Hawk.

Burnett had been the last one to the door. He stood in front of it now, his pistol in his hand, staring in shock and horror at the naked, blood-splattered Hawk. The rogue lawman stepped off the battered bed, shouldering away a corner of the fallen canopy.

Hawk curled his upper lip at Burnett.

As though he just now realized he was holding the pistol, Burnett snapped his pistol up. As he tightened his finger on the trigger, he jerked forward and fired the Merwin & Hulbert into the floor halfway between himself and Hawk.

Burnett screamed, staggered forward, and dropped to his knees.

A wooden-handled Bowie knife protruded from his back.

Jennie Broyles walked in behind him, clad in blue denims and a red and white checked wool shirt, her hair pulled back into a horse tail. Dixie, dressed similarly, walked into the room behind Jennie.

The women stood to either side of the raging saloon owner, who tipped his head back and gave a bellowing cry as he reached over his shoulder and pulled the knife out of his back. He tossed the knife on the floor and looked in pain and horror first at Jennie Broyles and then at Dixie.

"You... you... bitch!" Burnett bellowed.

Dixie smiled down at him, but there was no humor in her eyes. "Good riddance to you once and for all, Quentin. I hope the devil straps you with his oldest whore for all eternity."

Burnett jerked his gaze to Hawk. He looked around again, as though hoping to find someone remaining in the room who might offer assistance.

But there were only the two dead lawmen lying in thick, growing pools of their own blood and the two sobbing whores. The din of moments before had drifted downstairs, where the moneyed gamblers were apparently fleeing the building.

Hawk picked up an unfired shotgun and strode toward Burnett, mindless that he was naked. He looked like a savage—naked and blood-splattered. Saradee lay unmoving beneath the collapsed red canopy.

"Please don't shoot me," Burnett said, breathless, eyes pinched with pain.

"All right." Hawk tossed away the shotgun. Gritting

his teeth, he reached down, grabbed Burnett by his coat collar, and jerked the man to his feet.

Burnett bellowed miserably as Hawk dragged him savagely across the room and then hurled him through a window. The big saloon owner screamed as glass shattered around him.

There were several crunching thuds and yelps as Burnett rolled down a sloping roof.

Silence.

Another thud as Burnett hit the street out in front of the saloon.

Hawk walked over to the window. Jennie Broyles and Dixie moved to another window, to Hawk's left, and looked down into the street. Hawk could see Burnett lying in a pool of light cast by the Inn's first-story windows.

He was the only one on the street, the gamblers and other clientele apparently having fled the bloody violence. The only sounds were distant dogs barking and Burnett moaning as he lay on his back in the street. A slender, dark, hatted figure in a shapeless coat walked up to Burnett.

"Jacob," Jennie said, placing her hands against the window.

Then she swung around and ran out of the room. Dixie followed her.

Hawk looked back down into the shadowy, lamplit street. Jacob looked straight ahead, pricking his ears to get his bearings.

"Please," Burnett said between moans, raising a hand toward the slender, blind boy standing over him. "Help me!"

Jacob reached behind him and pulled what appeared to be a knife from the back of his belt. The boy crouched over Burnett. Hawk grinned as he saw the boy making a sweeping motion across the top of Burnett's forehead with the knife.

Burnett squealed like a gutshot javelina.

Jacob's knife worked deftly for a brief time. Then he straightened and held up something small and dark and ragged-edged and dripping. Burnett's scalp.

Burnett squealed again, louder, clutching his head in his hands.

"Look, sis," Jacob said, turning toward the Inn's veranda. "I got the first hide for the wall of our new cabin!"

Hawk had to chuckle at that.

"What's so damn funny?"

He whipped around and jerked his startled gazed toward the canopy-draped bed. Saradee sat on the edge of the bed, massaging her throat with both hands and looking over her shoulder at Hawk.

"You 'bout killed me." She worked her jaws, clearing her throat. "Like to have snapped my neck!"

"No," Hawk said, dully.

Saradee rose slowly and walked toward Hawk in all her naked splendor, hips rolling, jutting breasts jostling.

"No," Hawk said, shaking his head in disbelief. "No. I killed you. Once and for all, I killed you."

"If you'd wanted to, lover," Saradee said, reaching up and wrapping her arms around his neck. "If you'd really wanted to, you would have."

She kissed him tenderly, then gazed lovingly up into his face. "What do you say we round up our duds and head downstairs? I could use a drink. I got a sneaking feelin' we're gonna have the whole place to ourselves. That's a lot of busthead, lover!"

"No," Hawk said again, still shaking his head. "No."

He blinked his eyes as though to clear them. "No. No. You're not here. You're a dream."

"If I was," Saradee said, pressing her lips to his once more and lifting his hands to her breasts, "I'd be one hell of one—wouldn't I?"

*A LOOK AT ROGUE LAWMAN BOOK
NINE: UNDERTAKER'S FRIEND*

BY PETER BRANDVOLD

**SADDLE UP AND JOIN GIDEON HAWK ON HIS
SEARCH FOR JUSTICE ON THE TRAILS OF THE
WESTERN FRONTIER.**

Gideon Hawk shoots three men who try to rob the saloon he's
drinking in. One of those men is the spoiled son of a local
rancher, Mortimer Stanley. The rancher doesn't take kindly to
Hawk killing his son despite the crime his son was committing.

When the rancher sends five men into town to kill Hawk, and
Hawk turns them all toe-down, dead as stones, war clouds
gather over the little prairie town of Cedar Bend.

"Action-packed...for fans of traditional westerns."—**Booklist**

AVAILABLE April 2022

Peter Brandvold grew up in the great state of North Dakota in the 1960's and '70s, when television westerns were as popular as shows about hoarders and shark tanks are now, and western paperbacks were as popular as *Game of Thrones*.

Brandvold watched every western series on television at the time. He grew up riding horses and herding cows on the farms of his grandfather and many friends who owned livestock.

Brandvold's imagination has always lived and will always live in the West. He is the author of over a hundred lightning-fast action westerns under his own name and his pen name, Frank Leslie.